BIG WATER:

REVENGE — BOUNTY

BY
EUGENE ARNOLD

VOLUME IV IN A SERIES CHRONICLING THE LIFE AND ADVENTURES OF BRUCE COGGINS

A NOVEL OF 19TH CENTURY FLORIDA

This work of fiction, fourth in a series, is entirely the product of the author's imagination. While the setting for the story, and surrounding historic descriptions of places and circumstances are authentic, any resemblance of the characters in this book to any person, living or dead, is unintended and is purely coincidental.

ISBN: 1-891118-26-9

All Drawings by Wes Siegrist

Layout & Cover Work
By
Wind Canyon Publishing, Inc.
P.O. Box 1445
Niceville, FL 32588

MANUFACTURED IN THE UNITED STATES OF AMERICA

Other books by this author:

BIG WATER: FLIGHT TO OKEECHOBEE
(ISBN 0-9628828-2-8) Prospector Press, 1992

BIG WATER: WEST TO THE EVERGLADES
(ISBN 0-9628828-4-4) Prospector Press, 1993

BIG WATER: RANGE BOUNDARIES — UNKNOWN
(ISBN 1879630-42-7) Wind Canyon Publishing, Inc.

Copies of above books or additional copies of —

BIG WATER: REVENGE — BOUNTY

may be ordered directly from the author at the following address. Please enclose a check or money order for $6.95 for each copy desired. There is no charge for shipping, but Florida residents please add 7% sales tax.

Mail orders to:

Eugene Arnold
23 Canal Way BHR
Okeechobee, FL 34974

BIG WATER:

REVENGE — BOUNTY

A NOVEL OF 19TH CENTURY FLORIDA

TABLE OF CONTENTS

CHAPTER 1

Burl Collins was not a bad name, especially when it was used only as an alias. He disliked having to use it, even though it had saved Bruce Coggins from returning to Raiford prison in handcuffs at the front end of a gun by a reward-hungry bounty hunter, where he would serve the balance of his sentence with more time added to pay for his escape.

Washing the name away in the waters of the Caloosehatchee River when leaving the mullet fishermen at Tice, Bruce knew he was finished with it. And when a man came by boat to his fishing dock and introduced himself as Wade Range, the local representative of the Florida Cattlemen's Association, where he addressed Bruce as Burl Collins, Bruce knew it was no mistake, but deliberate to inform him that he knew of his past and what Bruce could expect if he refused to cooperate.

Wade did not have to elaborate on the name he called Bruce to get the message across. It was delivered and Bruce was aware of where Wade had obtained the information.

With Wade carrying the ball at that point, Bruce

remained silent to hear Wade explain their need of him to help break up a gang of cattle rustlers who had about bankrupted some of the ranchers.

Lending an attentive ear to Wade's plan of operation to capture the rustlers, Bruce agreed to help, but knew he would operate according to his own thinking.

At the time of the rustlers' capture in the cattle holding pen, the multicolored Indian shirt Bruce was wearing along with his using the English language in the manner Indians do, and his companion dressed the same, they had Wade hoodwinked about Bruce's true identity — but not the two rustlers who made their getaway on fast horses.

Leaving the Association men and ranchers befuddled after they were thought to be in cahoots with the rustlers, the two look-like Indians rode toward a descending late afternoon sun, where they camped in the first suitable hammock they reached that provided grazing nearby for their horses.

Settled in for the night, Fannie lay relaxed on her bedroll awaiting sleep while listening to creatures of the forest who were heard only at night: raccoons were in camp fussing over the few morsels of food discarded from the hastily prepared supper, while deep in the forest a hoot owl made its first call of the night.

Bruce lay there thinking about the two rustlers who escaped on fast horses at the holding pen. He had noticed their exerted interest when seeing him, indicating they thought they had seen him before. And he was positive he had seen them before. This was now bedeviling Bruce to no end. Even though he was weary from hard work, sleep would not come.

Some time after midnight, his rolling and twisting in a half-asleep stupor while changing positions awoke Fannie where she inquired of his problem. And at that instant the tension snapped.

Bruce now remembered. The men were two of the hard-core prisoners of Raiford who had tried to organize a mass prison break, and became angry with him when he refused to join them. Now they would be especially angry after he had managed to escape alone. His thoughts were, "If they remember who I am, I certainly will have to begin sleeping with one eye open."

Sun rays were filtering through the hammock when Fannie decided Bruce had enough sleep and nudged him awake to have a bit of breakfast before they were back in the saddle to be on their way.

Even with driving their mounts hard, it was mid-afternoon when they arrived at the livery stable in Tantie to turn in their two rented horses, before walking to the Kissimmee River to cross on the ferry to reach Buckhead Ridge at dusk.

Now, back with their friends, Bruce's plans were to get back to fishing with his two Indian partners. But again tonight there was no sleep. Then, after what seemed hours, recalling his memory of these two men (they were long term prisoners of Raiford), Bruce knew they had not been released after their sentence. "They must have escaped," he thought.

With a tormented mind keeping him awake, Bruce thought, "When they remember that I am the boy who would not help them organize the escape, and then managed to do it alone, only to join up with lawmen to capture them, it certainly will make them love me!"

Finally, after a few hours sleep, with a hastily prepared trail pack, daybreak found Bruce on foot beyond Tantie heading toward the rustlers' holding pen.

Reaching the pen with the sun now tangled with the tree tops, there had been no rain since he was there and sign of the escaping prisoners was still visible.

With the escape route located, Bruce sat to lean against a tree and rest a bit while pondering the situation. "Knowing now that I am in the area, if they are not captured, after escaping the lawmen on their trail, the two rustlers will be back here searching for me," Bruce was thinking. "There is only one safe way for me — make sure they are captured. But I will have to manage it without being seen, lest they will blow the whistle on me as an escapee. They have so much head start. But if I could reconstruct their thoughts and actions in my mind, maybe I could gain back some of that lost time." Moving away with long strides, he added, "Maybe not, but I can try!"

CHAPTER 2

Ignoring heat produced by a late summer sun, hanging at a quarter angle in mid-afternoon as it descended slowly toward the western horizon, and with the signs of a hard day of working with cattle plainly visible on man and beast, four horsemen had their mounts pointed toward the east in a fast run.

These men were not riding as a group. They were in pairs and separated by a few hundred yards, although the two bringing up the rear while pushing hard to narrow the space between themselves and the others, would have liked nothing better than riding as a foursome if the front two could have been in handcuffs. But the chance of accomplishing this would be remote.

The lead pair, having the advantage of a head start to put this space between themselves and their pursuers (with it generally known that those with everything to lose will exert greater effort to avoid capture) this distance was gradually increasing.

Gaining a head start with their surprise dash for freedom, after realizing the game was now over and they would, in a very short time, be on their was back to the state prison at Raiford, the large and small outlaws, who were out front and demanding every ounce of energy their mounts were able to produce, were in no mood to be captured at this time.

When making their sudden break from the group at the rustlers' secret holding pen in a dense sable palm hammock near Kissimmee, where they were a part of the organized rustling operation, the two who recently had escaped from the state prison, left their temporary captors, riders of the Florida Cattlemen's Association — who had finally solved the long and stubborn case — sitting in their saddles watching them ride off, before it dawned on them that they, too, were supposed to blast off in hot pursuit of the "long loop" operators.

Two years of long, hard hours were spent — with a great portion of that time in the saddle — by riders of the Cattlemen's Association, while trying to protect their members before this day of finally capturing the phantom gang red handed. These were cunning and elusive thieves who had about bankrupted some of the outfits along their range of operation. Upon apparently capturing these four men, the two who were escapees from prison were now trying for another break, leaving their partners, owners of two "scrub" one-man spreads in the lower Alapattah Flats area, to fight the battle alone. This was the day the Association men had waited so long for. It seemed the stubborn case was about to come to a close.

After much hard work for the past two weeks while trying to increase the number of cattle in the holding pen to a paying-size herd by scrapping a few head from each of the ranches in the area, the rustlers were captured on the last day before they planned to leave at daybreak for the long drive across the state to the small village of Ruskin, where the cattle would be loaded on flatboats to

6

be transferred to an ocean-going ship which was anchored offshore in Tampa Bay to receive the cargo, before departing for the Caribbean Islands.

It was well after mid-day when the rustlers were suddenly surprised by the appearance of the other riders and the capture was made. After inspection of the cattle, proof of ownership was established that connected the two renegade ranchers with stolen cattle.

The sun was tilting very low in the west, but seeming to be hanging immobile, favoring the fleeing horsemen, before descending further toward the earth.

With the two riders of the Association, who were ordered to fall in behind the fast horsemen, pushing their mounts hard to overhaul the rustlers before darkness set in, they were becoming discouraged to see they were gaining no ground. And when twilight made their pursuers invisible, the fast riding outlaws began veering from the due east course by angling toward the southeast for a spell before abruptly changing to ride toward the northeast, hoping the sudden changes in course would assist them in evading a sure addition to the remaining part of a sentence they left behind when escaping, if they lost this race.

By continuing this method of zigzagging to evade capture, the outlaws were also taking a long chance of straying from their general course and not reaching the point they were heading for. But even when darkness overtook them and the gentle breeze which reached this far inland from the ocean ceased to be noticeable, the moist perspiration on their faces detected a tinge of freshness when pointed in that direction and kept them on course.

Losing sight of their quarry after darkness arrived, the Association's men were also using the feel of the cool night air to follow. But when reaching the first point where the outlaws changed course, their horses showed reluctance to continue. This appeared to be the end of the chase and the men were about ready to acknowledge defeat and turn back when, after a brief hesitation, their mounts showed willingness to continue if allowed to change course. When the riders let their horses exercise their animal instincts, they were again on the trail of the other horses, but in a different direction, but now the space between them and the rustlers was greater than before.

Carrying on into the night, with the lead pair of riders stopping occasionally for a brief moment to listen for sound of the riders behind them, this fox and hound type chase was rapidly covering mile after mile, but even with the stops of the front pair to make sure if they were still on the wanted list, no ground was gained by the pursuers. They, too, were tarrying while waiting for their mounts to find and follow each new change in course.

Actions of all horses — both those of the pursuers and the pursued — were showing signs of wear when a full moon rose above the tops of the tall pines, to display dark patches of perspiration about their mounts necks and shoulders, causing the men to realize rest for the animals must be coming soon, regardless of the outcome of the chase.

As time passed, with all glamour of the contest long ago spent, while penetrating ever deeper into the forests toward the east, the lawmen were hoping the escapees would suspect they had gotten away clean and become careless by stopping or slowing their pace.

Riding stubbornly onward with this in mind, the lawmen were exercising caution to avoid making unnecessary sound and, unwittingly, defeating themselves because this was slowing their pace and they were getting farther behind.

With the four horsemen traveling farther into the night, they had covered many miles and were getting closer to the coast where the landscape was changing from sable palm hammocks and cypress strands, to higher land with mostly dense growths of scrub palmetto covering wide areas between towering oaks with moss-draped branches. Then occasionally, there were small sunken areas where sweet bay trees, covered with large white blossoms grew close, creating an almost impenetrable jungle which had to be crossed or find passage around.

Crossing this area and going farther east, the landscape and ground surface began changing again. There was flat, treeless land with some places covered with shallow water and with an abundant growth of cattails and sawgrass.

It was in one of the large and deeper sawgrass-covered, water areas which lay long across their route and had to be crossed, that the two rustlers who were now a considerable distance out front and slashing incautiously along in the water while trying to avoid the sharp saw-edged grass, disturbed a monstrous mother alligator that was guarding her nest of large, elongated eggs which she had placed upon a sizable mound of dried debris to be hatched into tiny lizard-like reptiles by the heat of the summer sun.

When they stumbled over the sleeping mama gator, she was totally surprised, but not more than were the horses and riders. The sudden event, along with the swiftness of the horses, prevented time for the attack which mama would liked to have made, but no time at all was needed for her to become extremely angry. And when the next pair of riders came along a few minutes later, mama was everything but asleep. She heard the horses pushing their way noisily along the exact route of the others and was ready.

To contact less of the knife-like grass the horses walked single file while in the pond, and if mama gator had done her thing when the first horse reached her, she could have spilled both riders practically on top of her by causing their mounts to become frightened and act spasmodically, parting company with their unsuspecting riders. But because of her anger she was a bit anxious and

moved prematurely, resulting in the lead horse seeing and springing to jump clear over her and bolt forward with no thought of sawgrass or anything else, while its rider desperately pulled leather to stay aboard.

The sudden actions of the lead horse and sight of the big gator now standing upright on its back feet while balancing with its tail pressing against the ground, and with the sound of the gnashing of its sharp teeth only a half dozen feet in the trail ahead, caused the back horse to act with lightening speed and rear up to also stand on its back legs. But not at all with the thought of attacking the gator. This was the fastest way of getting its body heading back the way they came. This sudden and surprising action dumped the rider who landed on his seat in the thick growth of tall wiry-edged grass growing in knee-deep water, almost within an arm's length and directly in front of a powerhouse of anger.

Sometimes one can move fast, and there are other times when even that speed record has to be broken. And with mama gator like a bolt of lightening in overdrive using extreme energy to reach the point where the man-thing sat in the water, when she reached that point he was no longer there, but twenty feet away on his hands and feet clawing at the sawgrass or anything that would help to pull himself along faster while pushing the sand bottom of the pond with his feet, creating a turbulence equal to that of the propeller of a tugboat, while on the course of his fleeing horse, and with mama only a short distance behind.

When realizing the seriousness of his partner's position, the other rider quickly turned his mount to race back and allow the grounded man to swing up on the horse's rump behind him, but not before the seat of the man's pants was left hanging between the jaws of a fast-closing

11

vise.

Moving erratically from the pond with mama trying desperately to trip the overloaded horse and dump the riders, they finally reached dry land to find the frightened and nervous horse waiting near the pond, not knowing if it still had a master.

There were no intentions on the part of these two Association men of losing half the rustling gang after so much hard work was involved in finally catching them in the act. They knew that the two rustlers would be as hard pressed for rest and sleep as they were and somewhere ahead, after thinking they were the winners of the chase, would stop for rest and become sitting ducks. Anyway, if it took a week to run the men down, they planned to be present at the count-down seven days from then.

But without being aware of the advantage of the distance gained during the commotion in the pond between the pursuers and a creature which didn't give a hoot whether the intruders were lawmen or just plain long-loop cattle thieves, the lawmen were still close on the trail. The rustlers started pushing even harder than before.

And while drifting deeper into the night with distance flowing smoothly under their faithful horses gently swaying bodies and fast moving feet, the foremost thought in the minds of the two leading horsemen, was hoping their opponents would tire and turn back before the sun gave light of another day.

Long before any sign of daybreak could be detected, while the landscape began changing again to higher ground with large oaks demanding a place among the more plentiful sable palms which were now not confined to clusters, but scattered every place, and tall pines shading clusters of scrub palmetto, unnatural illumination could be faintly detected at the tops of trees which towered over a thick growth of others below, causing a sudden awareness of danger and calling for extreme caution as the two rustlers brought their mounts to a walking pace while approaching the light, only a quarter mile ahead. Only fire could be causing the reflection in the treetops, but why a fire in this remote section, far removed from any civilization? As men who had spent more nights on the ground under stars than inside under a roof, they knew the reflection was due to one of two causes: the remnants of a past forest fire could be lingering in the thick growth of trees to finish off the remains of a decaying log, or was the fire of campers, past or present?

The latter possibility gave food for thought. If campers were there now, would they be friend or foe? With this question in mind, the two horsemen who were now a considerable distance ahead of the lawmen, continued toward the light with caution. They saw the reflection in the trees grow brighter as they came closer.

Reaching the thick fringe of the large cluster of trees, after slowing their pace to that of a tortoise while exercising extreme caution, more light in a small clearing near the center of the hammock could be seen where flames leaped lively upward at a few seconds intervals from glowing embers of a dying campfire, causing light reflection in the treetops to change with each flare-up, and to illuminate for brief periods, a silent camp of sleeping men.

After leaving their mounts ground-hitched outside the hammock and stealthily finding their was among the trees to reach a clear area with the fire near its center, the dark prone images of a dozen or more men were visible where they lay surrounding the fire a few feet away, but with their bodies pointing in all directions, while in various stages of slumber. Loud snores were coming from some while others, occasionally, made different sounds.

The rustlers and their horses were also needing rest and would have been extended a friendly welcome if the camp had been reached before these men retired, but to awaken anyone to ask permission to share the camp would surely arouse everything but friendliness.

Upon closer observation the acrid odor of human sweat mixed with other, occasional, fumes along with large hats lying near their bodies, branded these men cowpokes on an extended cow hunt and the rustlers knew that under normal conditions this would be a friendly group. But on the other hand, it would not be considered normal for strangers to enter camp after midnight and awaken the occupants just to ask permission to sleep on the free earth.

Backing quietly away from the sleeping men and going around the hammock to continue on their way, the rustlers found the cow hunters' horses staked out to graze in a small prairie near the hammock. In the cunning minds of these two, an idea was born. They lost no time in pulling the saddles from their mounts and staking them among the others. And after stashing their saddles in some nearby bushes, they sneaked quietly back to bed down with the sleeping cowpokes, while expecting at any moment to hear the Association men barging into camp.

With fatigue now most dominant, only a short period of time passed, with the rustlers fast asleep and their appearance the same as that of the other men, when they were awakened by loud and boisterous talking. Remaining motionless and feigning sleep while listening to the seemingly one-sided conversation, they heard the ramrod of the camping cowhunters loudly saying in an angry tone of voice with well-spaced and biting words,

"Listen, fellows! Don't you two lard heads give us credit for having at least enough intelligence to know if rustlers had visited with us, or even came near this camp tonight? I am not at all concerned with your claim of being representatives of the Florida Cattlemen's Association! You could just as well tell me you two are the Governor and his Lieutenant, or even the President for what effect it will have on us! And I'm telling you, Buster, we have our job to do, and it ain't hunting cow thieves! Now, back them nags out of this hammock and stop disturbing my men!"

With no further discussion necessary, the riders left the sleeping camp and rounded the hammock toward the east, where they found the group of horses tethered in the prairie of lush grass. And while having to pass close to the animals, they noticed two of them acting differently than the others. These two were biting the tall grass ravenously, while all the others stood in a dropped-hip, relaxed form, sleeping.

Passing on for a few yards, one of the men quickly stopped his horse and turned back. He rode close beside one of the feeding horses and felt its back, to find it wet with perspiration and the hair slicked down where a saddle had only a short time before been removed from the animal. Finding the other suspicious member of the pair the same way, while all the others were dry, left only one answer to the mystery.

Knowing now that the cowman either lied to them or the rustlers were smarter than given credit for, and were using this ruse to give their horses an opportunity to rest and feed while they, too, holed up someplace in the brush for a few hours to let them pass, thinking they were still on the thieves' trail.

The rustlers' smartness was now becoming evident.

15

But the lawmen themselves were not without the ability to scheme. Medicine good for the Indian would also benefit his Squaw. So they rode on noisily toward the east for a few hundred yards before stopping to wait for a short period of time, then returning silently to place their horses among the others, before taking comfortable positions in the thick foliage at the edge of the hammock where they were in visual command of the horses and the surrounding area.

When realizing, after hearing the questions asked the head man of the cow hunters by the lawmen, and his answers given, that they were genuinely suspicious and not at all satisfied with the foreman's answer, the rustlers knew their pursuers would not give up at this point, and it would not be safe to remain in the camp, only to be discovered and possibly captured. And also believing the lawmen had not traveled on after leaving the disgruntled cowman, but would be on their tail again when light would allow, left them only one course of action.

The rays of a high and hot sun filtering through the forest of tall pines awakened and brought two surprised lawmen from cover, where fatigue had been master causing them to unwittingly fall asleep. Finding themselves to be alone and with only two horses grazing where there were many, gave the sleepyheads a feeling of stupidity, but what was done would simply have to be past history and they would try to not let it bother them.

Quickly leaving their place of concealment while carrying their saddles, they went to where the two horses were now standing in a position of relaxation, to mount up and get back after the rustlers with no more lost time. But when reaching the animals it was found these were

16

not the two they had been riding. One discreditable strike against their dignity could have been tolerated, but compounding the insult was more than the lawmen cared to put up with. This was one of their neat tricks that the rustlers were going to regret. But for now there was no option and no time to ponder the situation. The lawmen simply saddled what was available and mounted hurriedly to ride out.

With a heavy dew of the past night still lying on the tall grass of the prairie, the direction followed by the other riders when leaving was obvious. A large portion of them had gone south, while a trail in the disturbed dew showed plainly where only two had chosen to be different. They were heading directly toward the rising sun.

Following the bold sign toward the east, the lawmen were elated with the faster pace they were able to make in daylight, and with not knowing how much of a head start their quarry had, they were encouraged by the possibility of soon overhauling them.

But while following the bold sign with the greatest of ease, the sun was extending ever higher, and wind of the day sprang up to gradually increase and destroy the heavy blanket of wet dew, leaving the men without sign to follow, and seriously hampering their efforts to gain ground. But not so with the outlaws. They knew where they were going and needed no trail to follow.

When the visible trail finally ended, the lawmen became desperate and drove their new mounts unreasonably hard, hoping to overtake the rustlers before reaching the coastal area where there was a greater concentration of residents and more activity, making it easier for sign left by the two thieves to mix with that of local horsemen, to be absorbed and lost completely. And as they traveled onward, with the heat of the sun increasing, this thought

brought frustration, causing the deputies to realize their efforts may be in vain and the entire time wasted.

But with not allowing one discouraging incident to destroy the cause of "Law and Order" they pushed doggedly on and on, for mile after mile to reach and cross a chain of Savannas where there was various depths of water, with large lily pads spread flat on the surface, where monstrous bass and bluegills were lurking in residence below, and with water moccasins sunning them-

18

selves atop the broad leaves of the plants or anything else that would support the weight of their heavy bodies. Mud turtles and sizable alligators were seen sliding off floating tufts of live vegetation into the murky black water.

After crossing the wetlands, sand hills immediately began showing up, supporting dwarf oak and hickory trees, and with the never-ending ground cover of a knee-deep growth of vines which bore pods of tiny black grapes.

The tangled vines on this white and infertile ground made walking difficult for the horses even without having to be on the constant lookout for spiny prickly pear cactus which protruded up through the vines in a sneaky way to make themselves hard to see, not to mention the large diamondback rattlers which dozed quietly in a coil under the vines, waiting patiently for a dinner of mice, birds, rabbits or any creature a bit smaller than a horse, which may come for grapes.

When reaching and trying to navigate this unfamiliar and unyielding landscape, considerable extra time was necessary for the lawmen to pick their way through the entanglement at nearly the pace of a scaly sand lizard. And with the sun now at the top, as they struggled to make headway, seemingly to add to the present unusual situation with another surprise, the sound of a steam whistle was heard in the near distance ahead.

The sound of the whistle coming from this land of oddities was entirely unexpected and tended to momentarily frighten. But with having heard steam whistles at sawmills, the lawmen knew what to expect ahead.

Knowing now that they were nearing civilization and would have to make every minute count, extra effort was applied in driving their horses even harder that they might catch the escapees before the chance of bringing

them to justice would be lost forever.

After hearing the whistle and pushing on a bit farther, the lawmen could see a large, weathered, cypress
wood water tank silhouetted against the skyline above the
tops of scrub hickory and bent dwarf pine trees a short
distance ahead. The tank was tall and a large crooked
pipe came out the bottom to project upward along the
tank's side.

As they made their way through the vines to finally
reach the tank, they found it stood close beside the tracks

of a railroad. On the tracks and under the tank, the ground was wet, showing where a large quantity of water was spilled within the hour. And far to the south a red caboose was seen to disappear around a bend in the tracks. Still farther down the line, the whistle of a steam locomotive was heard to blast as it approached another grade crossing with a hundred freight cars ahead of the caboose.

With now losing no time wondering about the purpose of the water tank's position so near the tracks, and knowing they would be able to follow sign of the other horses in the soft white sand of the area, the lawmen quickly crossed the tracks to continue the search of the outlaws. It was not until then that they saw the two saddled and riderless animals nibbling contentedly at the sparse and short grass a short distance from the tracks and tank.

CHAPTER 3

There had been no rain since the four horsemen passed this way, and with Bruce's Indian training there was no problem with following sign. He now was in the hammock where the escapees bedded down with the cowpokes, and with sign of so much commotion, wondered if they had been captured at that point and were now on their way to prison, somehow getting past him on their way.

Thirty days in jail was the usual sentence given common bums for vagrancy after they refused to take a job of honest toil, or for overly ambitious cowpokes and trouble-bent mullet fishermen who liked to show their superiority and marksmanship on the streets of the little cattle and commercial fishing town of Fort Pierce, usually on Saturday night. And so it was for enjoying the comfort of a ride on freight trains without the permission of its owner.

This old cowboy whom the sight of was familiar to everyone, and who was in town today, had long passed sixty summers of riding the prairies from Fort Drum, Bassenger, Noccatee, Arcadia and Fort Ogdon before deciding this Indian river town had more to offer lonely off-duty wranglers. He had lived in this area for the past ten years.

The old bowlegged and warped waddie had rode for many outfits, but still had not exhausted his usefulness, nor his desire for a bit of pleasure and recreation. He made the town once a month to blow his thirty dollars pay. He could always be depended on to find a fight with someone — anyone — before his bankroll was gone. He was extremely lucky to receive a sentence so short for his actions this time.

He had been involved in a shoot-out with the town's "Dandy" for vocally admiring the Dandy's girlfriend as they passed him, where he stood on the wooden sidewalk leaning against a hitch rail for a better view of all foot traffic which may pass that way. The old cowpoke's ancient six-shooter proved a bit too fast for the man with his girl, sending both scurrying for cover behind the batwing entrance of the Buckhorn saloon.

And with his gun hand warmed up, he was now ready to take on the entire town. But the old waddie was not long in learning there were men of his equal when suddenly the saloon doors burst open allowing the Sheriff to pile out with a pair of blazing guns to make spurts of sand dance about the cowboy's feet, where he now stood in a gunman's stance at the center of the crossing of two dirt streets. This action of fun cost the old boy thirty days.

Fort Pierce was a town many would look back at, although it was larger than many others along the Florida east coast at the turn of the century. It was a four-street town, with two narrow dirt streets running north and south, while two others pointed the other way. The town covered the entire area between the west bank of the sprawling Indian river and a hundred yards beyond the newly installed railroad for its east and west boundaries. But if you wanted to cover the town the other way, you would have to go all the way from Moore's creek on the north to the new rail depot at the south end — a distance of over a quarter mile.

The old cowboy's sentence was well on its way to a finish when two tough men in their thirties, one larger than the other, were pushed roughly into the jail cell with him.

It was only after the commotion was over and the new prisoners turned from watching the Sheriff and jailer return to the ground floor, that they saw the cowboy sitting on his bunk in the darker part of the cell. He sat silently and motionless through the jailing of these two, but now with each of them selecting a bunk for themselves and slouching on it, he was first to indicate friendliness by trying to converse with them.

After leaving the hammock where the escapees bedded down with the cowboys, sign was clear and Bruce was able to cover ground more rapidly. Arriving at the Savannas in late afternoon to cross and reach the water tank and railroad, Bruce found the sign he had followed to be no more. And while searching the area he heard a steam whistle toward the north. Then a freight train rounded a curve and stopped at the water tank. This solved the puzzle! The men had caught a train at this point, but in which direction? With a fifty-fifty chance of going in the right direction, he would catch this one now. After finding an empty boxcar with open doors a short distance behind the engine, Bruce climbed up and sat with his feet hanging out the door.

The engine taking on water from the tank did not take long and the train was on its way again, to arrive and

stop in Fort Pierce where a lawman greeted Bruce with, "Indian, you must be new at riding freights. Experienced hobos will always go to the dark end of a boxcar when the train reaches town. Come with me."

The people of Fort Pierce could boast of having a two-cell jail, and the empty one next to where the escapees and cowboy were is where the lawman put Bruce. He was not seen by the others when brought in and he now sat quietly listening to their talk.

The newcomers in the cell with the old cowboy were not in any mood for idle talk, but after being alone for the better part of a month, the cowboy was starved for conversation and would welcome it from any source. He lost no time in searching for some subject they would respond to. After trying various approaches from trying to discuss the weather, to cow hunting, branding and jailhouse grub with no success, he finally casually mentioned that he believed if he could squeeze through the jail bars he would hit the imaginary "Wild Boar Trail" toward the west and never be heard of around these parts again. This immediately brought new life to two very much bewildered individuals.

Without delay the largest of the new prisoners came and sat on the bunk beside the cowboy to ask, "Is there really a trail such as you are talking about? Or maybe you are just wishing there was!"

"Shore, the trail is there. I've heard tell of it off and on for the better part of my life!" the cowboy quickly said with enthusiasm over gaining attention of his cellmates.

"Since you are so sure about this trail, who uses it? And where does it lead to?"

"Oh, that trail!" the old fellow followed with, after a short pause and seeming to suddenly realize what the subject was about. "But you wouldn't want to follow it," he added. "That trail is only used by cattle thieves, murderers and bank robbers, when the Sheriff gets too close on their tail and they have to leave town fast!" Then after another brief pause, the old man hastily added, "I've hear'n tell that if you know how to follow the trail, you can make your way all the way to Texas 'thout gettin caught!"

"How about the lower west coast of Florida? Will it take a man in that direction, too?" the man asked with renewed interest.

"I've hear'n it'll take you just about any place you want to go!" Then adding, "But you got to know how to read sign if you want to stay on the trail!"

The big prisoner was now noticeably eager to hear more of what the cowpoke was telling him, but when hearing that only one trail was needed to reach anyplace, he could not understand how this was managed, and was in doubt of his benefactor's veracity. But with nothing to lose by learning more, he moved forward to sit on the extreme edge of the bunk and face the old man while ask-

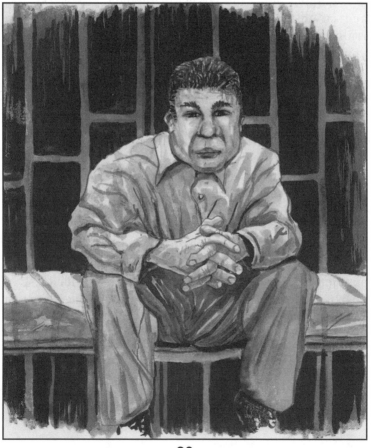

ing, "Where does this trail start? Could you find its beginning?"

"Shore I could find it! It starts rat here on the west edge of town!"

"Why did the trail have to start on the edge of this town? Why could it not have started near some other town?"

"Well, doggone, Buster. Everybody knows it is needed most near this town!"

All this time the other new, and smaller, prisoner had said nothing. He was listening to the conversation in silence but was by no means idle. He was busily working with his hands, where a wire clothes hanger was already twisted to form a strong frame body, which ran through the holes on the ends of a new hacksaw blade, creating an effective tool. And he was now testing his ingenious work of art for its workability on a cell bar near the floor under the end of a swing-up bunk bed.

As strokes of the saw made loud rasping sounds while moving to and fro across the hard iron bar, the man sitting on the bunk beside the old cowhand noticed it and was sure the sound could be heard downstairs. He began patting his foot on the floor and clapping his hands while chanting religious words in a spiritual tone of voice, and making sure to keep in exact rhythm with the actions of the saw, regardless of proper tune, which drowned out the constant and metallic sounds the saw was making.

In seeing this it took no major brain work for the cowboy to understand the men's intentions. Up until this point they had let him do most all the talking. He told them of the many times he had become overly playful while in town and had to pay for it by sitting a spell in this very cell, and why he was in this time. But he had learned nothing of their past. All he knew about them was the rattling of jail keys and the loud swearing which awoke him about daybreak that morning when they were pushed roughly into the cell with him. Then, after a short while, to hear one of them remark when hearing a freight train pulling out of town, "There goes our Pullman, Buddy!"

Bruce heard and silently agreed.

The cowboy knew what their plans were, but it didn't make sense to him. All he ever knew was a thirty-day stretch, and he was not about to have another year added to that for trying to break jail. Their actions put him to wondering. Why would they want to break out if they were only in for riding "blind baggage" on a freight train, which usually cost you only from ten to thirty days out of circulation if the jail was empty at the time? Otherwise, it was hoped you would ride quietly on out of town.

With the day now reaching high noon, three grub pans were pushed between the bars into the cell, but the trustee who brought the food heard nothing. The sawing had already ceased. One end of the inch-thick iron bar was sawed through and the second and final phase of the job would be started immediately after the food pans were collected, about an hour later, by the trusted prisoner who also did the cooking.

As time passed on into mid-afternoon, with work progressing satisfactorily on the section of bar to be removed, the two ruffians had become more communicative. They loosened up enough to tell their new-found friend they were escapees from the state prison at Raiford, and now with them picked for hoboling, if their identity was discovered, as quickly as someone from the prison could reach this town, they would be returned to finish their terms plus extra time for escaping. But that would be the route of an idiot. These hombres had other plans and strongly insisted on the cowboy going with them.

Up to this point Bruce thought he had recognized the voices which were coming from the other side of a solid steel panel between the cells. This clinched it. He felt lucky to be this close without their knowing. But, no, they were going to escape and he would still be here.

There are a great number of cowpokes who are not very bright, but the older ones have had more time to overcome part of that problem, and so it was with this simple-acting old fellow. He knew, after the other end of the cell bar was cut and freedom gained, locating the Wild Boar trail held top priority with these men, and when satisfied the beginning of the trail was reached, they would have no further use for him.

He remembered, too, how smoothly the saw blade was smuggled into the jail lying flat in the bottom of the large man's shoe, and thought it entirely possible for one or both the men to be packing a small hide-away gun which with his old faithful six-shooter held in the jail office until his release, would not give him a fair break. Using homespun evasive tactics all afternoon while the other end of the bar sawed through, but without definitely promising anything, the cowhand led the men to believe he would be going with them when the time came.

When supper was served in late afternoon all was quiet on the "jailbird front." The secret work was finished and everyone was relaxing in his bunk. Then, later, when the food pans were picked up while the day was fading into twilight, all conditions seemed normal.

Drifting up the stairwell from the kitchen, the sound of banging pots and pans together could be heard for awhile before it faded into nothingness as darkness outside grew deeper. Out the only window that gave a view from the cell, the outline of the old, crippled jailer could be seen sitting silently and still under a tree in his customary position of rest at day's end.

With darkness now complete and with an empty chair under the tree, only the dim kerosene light hanging in the walkway just outside the bars of the cell, gave any indication that there might be prisoners in residence.

Natural sounds of human activity downstairs drifted away while the cowboy went to bed as usual and the other two sat on their bunks waiting.

Then, when all lights on the ground floor were gone, the men were ready. They were anxious but knew time would have to be allowed for the trustee and jailer to be asleep. Not being able to wait any longer, they quietly moved from their bunks to start, but at that moment the twinkling of a dim light and footsteps were coming up the stairway.

Immediately one of the men lay back on the bunk in the dark part of the cell, directly over their handiwork underneath, while pretending to be retired for the night, with the other one quickly sitting back on his bed pretending to undress. But faking was not in the old cowboy's plans. He was in his bunk snoring — so they thought.

Hobbling to the front of the cell, the old crippled fellow held the lamp high to look in and check on the comfort of his prisoners. And when seeing one of them still awake, quietly asked if all was well. Agreeing that everything was shipshape except the lamp outside the cell bars, he said this would interfere with their sleep and asked that it be extinguished.

After the jailer had gone back downstairs and to his bedroom, enough time was allowed for him to be asleep before the swing-up bunk was raised to rest against the bars and both men crouched on the floor to apply pressure to the bar and break the small fragment of iron which was left to hold the bar in place so that it would not be noticed.

When a couple of husky tries were made to remove the sawed bar, but with no success, frustration began building and sweat flowed freely. And with the discouraging thought of possible failure rapidly increasing, one more extreme effort was made and the loose end of the bar came toward them a fraction of an inch, renewing their hopes.

As well as being not so bright, some cowhands can also be stubborn. And at the moment this was the case when much-whispered pleading for an extra hand failed. But sometimes in a case of life, death or freedom, a man's strength knows no bounds and this one last try brought the section of iron away entirely, leaving a gaping hole about one foot square in the network of the iron cage.

These two most jubilant men sat playfully pounding upon each other while eagerly whispering their happiness, as the sweat which had suddenly turned cold ran freely down their faces.

With the old cowhand now snoring more progressively, and after a short period of recovery with the other two, the short and thin escapee put his arms above his head and slithered through the opening in the style of a reptile, with the greatest of ease. But when the big man tried it and found his shoulders were too wide to even start through, the noisy anxiety which followed awakened their old friend.

To get the big man through with the ease in which the other made it would involve sawing out another bar, which they could do but it would mean staying over another day — and with not knowing if anyone was on the way from Raiford, to stay any longer was far beyond their desires.

With the section of bar removed there was a hole which would not escape discovery during the next routine cell inspection, and with their current run of luck not the best, along with there having been no inspection during the cowboy's stay this time, another day's delay was just asking for more trouble.

Anxiety was nearing the point of hysterics when the big man poked his head through the hole again, but with the same results. After pulling his head back in defeat, his body was trembling with anger and he was ready to try anything. He then put one arm through the hole first and found that his head would also pass through beside his arm. This brought on new encouragement, but when he tried to go farther the other shoulder stopped him.

Squatted beside the opening outside, offering suggestions and a generous amount of sympathy, the small prisoner's advice was more aggravating than helpful, which brought raised voices before they realized their noise could very easily get them captured.

Then when attempting to put the shoulder which was stopping him out of joint to make it smaller, by stretching his arm down beside his body as far as possible, the shoulder suddenly popped through the opening, leaving the bar pinning his arm tightly against his side.

This gimmick put the big man half in the cell and half out, plugging the hole entirely and with him genuinely stuck. He could not go either way, causing an unbelievable state of mind.

With much amusement, while faking sleep during the entire commotion, the cowboy's bed was now shaking

from uncontrollable, but stifled laughter.

And after a while of the little man pulling from the outside, the stuck man managed to move forward enough to free the arm which was wedged beside him, only to bring on further trouble — his big hips would not go through the hole.

Now this was a predicament neither had bargained for, and it brought spasmodic laughter from their cell-mate.

The next move to get the man through the hole was something else, for sure. He would not be able to put one leg up and the other down like he did with his arms to get his shoulders through, so they tried to get his hips through with the little man pulling from the upper end, outside, while the big man searched with his feet in the darkness behind him for something to push on.

While this method proved fruitless, the stuck man managed to loosen his belt by backing up a bit and reaching through other openings of the bars. But then he found he could not reach far enough to push his trousers down.

To call loud enough to awaken a lazy, sleeping cowpoke was next to impossible at any time. They knew this would be a major accomplishment but something had to be done, something had to give, and without delay.

The cowboy had managed to keep his fun to himself by not laughing loud enough for them to hear, and he was still pretending with loud snores between outbursts of choked laughter, when the man's voice, no louder than a rasping whisper, called pleadingly, "Cowboy! C-0-W-B-0-Y!"

Knowing the man to be genuinely stuck, the wrangler knew he was going to be called on for help, even before the big man called. While grumbling a bit to appear to be awakening, he sleepily said to the man, "What ails you, Buddy?"

"Pull my trousers down, quick!"

Laughter was now impossible for the cowboy to control, and with admitting to being awake there was no object in trying. But he did restrain it long enough to tell the distressed man, "Humph, nobody ever pulled mine down for me!" But even while saying this he was coming out of his bunk to help.

To make the man's hips smaller, even by the thickness of his pants, his pants were lowered to his feet and another try was made to free him from his highly embarrassing, if not impossible, position.

With his pants now down there was a little more progress. Sweat had lubricated his body, allowing his hips to go a bit farther, only to be wedged firmly between the bars.

The frustration this caused had no equal. With the man on the outside sitting on the floor bracing his feet against the bars while pulling on the stuck man's upper parts with all his strength, with the cowboy sitting helplessly at his rear, the big man frantically pleaded for the cowboy to, "Stretch the bars a little wider! Push! Do something! Anything!"

Wanting to help, but at a total loss for what to do, the cowboy tried the only thing that seemed practical. He placed his feet solidly against the big man's seat, and while gripping the bars for an anchor, gave a mighty push. This, along with the man outside pulling at the same time, caused a little more progress to be made — another inch of the man was on the outside.

The progress, even if slight, produced great encouragement and this was the method to use even with leaving small fragments of the man's skin clinging to the bars. But with the man stuck so firmly, this method failed the next time it was tried.

He tried twisting his body to lie on his side for more clearance, but this would not work because the hole was equal in size, both wide and high. Then with the cowboy's big feet still in place, they found when the man on the outside would pull the body sideways, the big man could feel his hip on the opposite side move forward a fraction of an inch.

This brought new hope and the big man's body was pulled the other way which resulted in the other hip coming forward to match, but with more skin left clinging to the bars.

The zigzagging method proved more effective than anything they had tried and would now be their tool.

After the body was pulled from side to side several times, each change making a little difference, both of the man's hips were finally on the outside, relieving the nerve tension of all concerned.

It now seemed the battle was over. But not quite. There was no way the two big feet and trousers would go through the hole together.

After losing a few minutes of precious time, while trying different possibilities, they learned that if the man pulled his trousers off over his feet he would then be able to bend one foot all out of shape and draw it through the opening beside the other leg, leaving space for the other foot to gain freedom.

This was a stroke of wisdom. There was nothing to stop their freedom now. To get the feet through the hole meant only a matter of a few seconds. But when attempting to reach his feet, still on the inside, he found it impossible. But again, this presented no problem, he would simply call on the cowboy to pull his pants off.

The comical acts of the big man while trying to remove his pants did not go unobserved. The cowpoke was sitting back on his bed now watching as best he could in the darkness and fully expected what he heard. "Come on, Cowboy! Pull 'em off!"

Quickly faking a long snore, which he knew would not mislead anyone, he tarried unreasonably long before coming forward while saying in a forced sleepy tone, "Hombre, who did you use for a pants jockey before breaking into my private jail?"

The big man was now on the outside, except for his trousers. Leaving them behind with a playful cowboy seemed to be a grave mistake, but there was no other way.

The big man wanted to believe the cowboy was kidding when he refused to push the pants where they could be reached through the bars, and became very angry before they were nudged slowly toward him. Then after grasping and while pulling them through the hole, he said to the cowboy with a voice laced in deceit, "Come on out, Pal! Let's get going!"

Calling him "Pal" would have been accepted at face value if spoken with a tone of sincerity, and before leaving the cell. But coming at this time, the old wrangler knew the length of that friendship was only from the jail to the beginning of the "Wild Boar Trail," where they would then be finished with him.

When he was pulling the trousers off over the big man's feet so that the big man would be able to get his feet through, the cowboy felt a small single-barrel derringer in a secret compartment sewn into the crotch, which was overlooked when the big man was searched before being locked up. The old fellow had lived long on the range, mostly by "unwritten law," and now felt pangs of guilt and dishonor, but he removed the little gun anyway.

The big man put his pants on without missing the gun, and now with a feeling of accomplishment after gaining freedom from the iron cage, and wanting to lose no time arguing with a stubborn half-baked cowpoke about accompanying them to point out the beginning of his imaginary escape trail, the escapees next problem was getting clear of the jail building undetected.

Both the trustee and the old jailer had bedrooms on the ground floor, and to go out through the front door the way they came in would be the riskiest route, but there seemed no option except the small window at the back of the room where the cell was located. With no rope, nor sheets or blankets from the bare bunks to tie together, the second floor window was just too high to jump from.

With the night still young, and knowing the jailer's bedroom and the jail office were just inside and to the right of the front door, they may have to wait awhile.

But the large escapee remembered that when they were booked in, the old fellow had to ask their names twice before understanding, and he had asked them to repeat or clarify other answers slowly, indicating that he had impaired hearing.

Contemplating the situation was a waste of precious time. They decided to take their chance through the route they were acquainted with. And without further ado about their new found friend going with them, they crept stealthily to the iron stairway and down to the first floor, where they paused to listen for sound before quietly unlocking the door and passing swiftly out into the night.

To reach the door they passed under the hanging kerosene light that had been extinguished earlier by the old jailer so they could sleep, but there was still just enough moonlight for Bruce to see them clearly as they passed his cell and he recognized them as the two he had known while serving time in Raiford.

The old cowhand had said the Wild Boar trail began at the west edge of town, and now with a full moon rising from the ocean, the two escapees had no problem knowing which way they wanted to go.

Sun rays were coming through the window when the sound of a tray against cell bars caught the old cowboy's attention, where he saw the cook begin placing food pans on the shelf, then to stop suddenly and ask, "Cowboy, where are your roommates?"

Drowsily, the old man said, "Uh, they had to leave!

Said they needed some fresh air!"

Leaving only one pan and quickly placing another on the shelf at Bruce's cell, the cook rushed from the cell block with two pans of food on his tray. Shortly, footsteps of the jailer and Sheriff were heard coming up the stairway. As they passed Bruce's cell to reach the cowboy, the Sheriff asked, "How did they get out of the cell?"

Pointing to the hole in the cell bars, the cowboy said, "Over there."

Looking at the hole where a section of only one bar was missing, the Sheriff said, "That hole is not large enough for a man to crawl through!"

"The big'un almost didn't," the old cowboy replied wryly.

"How did they make that hole?"

"The big one took a hacksaw blade from his shoe, just like the other man's shoes," answered the cowboy.

"Why didn't you call the jailer when you saw what they were doing?" the Sheriff demanded.

"Huh? And git my tail twisted?"

With an air of disgust the Sheriff turned to the jailer and said, "Put this old wrangler back in the saddle. He won't tell us anything, and has rested enough anyway!" Then, after a short pause, he added, "You might as well clear the jail completely. Feeding this Indian for thirty days ain't going to change his ways. He'll ride another freight train when he wants to come to town. But, wait a minute, Cowboy, what did you say about their shoes?"

"Oh, I said the big man and the little man wore shoes just alike, and was almost new."

"Did they say where they were going?"

"No, But when I told them about the "Wild Boar Trail," they wanted to know if would it take them to the lower west coast, where it began. I told them just west of town."

"Cowboy, don't you know that's nothing but a myth? There is no such trail!" the Sheriff said in a disgusted tone.

"Shore, it is out there, Sheriff. Everybody knows that! I've hear'n tell of it all my life," the cowboy answered while pointing his finger westward.

"Humph," the Sheriff mused as he went back downstairs.

Meanwhile, Bruce, who was listening attentively, had heard enough from the cowboy talking to the escapees and the Sheriff that locating where they left town and finding sign was minor for his trained eyes. He could hardly wait to get started.

CHAPTER 4

Sneaking rapidly along the narrow dirt street with only the sound of mountain air brushing gently against a boulder, the men felt confident. But there could yet be many obstacles to overcome. With the night just beginning they were extremely lucky that the inhabitants of this sleepy little town were in the habit of retiring to bed early. But what about yard dogs? Surely some of the residents of the houses they were passing would own them.

The town extended only a short distance to the west from the railroad before reaching a land of nothing but trouble. There were only a few houses on the street, and all had picket fences at the front of the lot bordering the street. While moving cautiously along the fence with no sound of suspicious dogs, they had nearly reached the point of cover they were heading for and feeling more confident with each step.

Now the feeling of being "home safe" increased as they passed silently under a large tree which grew in the front yard of the last house on the street, when suddenly they were startled by the noise of a flock of guinea fowl which were disturbed from their roosting place in the trees. Immediately the front door of the house opened slightly.

Crouching behind the three-feet high fence, the men moved as swiftly as possible on hands and feet, hoping to gain cover of the thick woods they could see ahead. But with the fence ending short of the woods, when they reached its end there would still be about one hundred feet of "no man's land" which they would have to cross.

They could see the end of the fence before reaching it but there was no time for planning. They simply had to take their chance, and they crossed the open space like a baseball player sliding into base. As they loudly crashed into the thick growth of scrub palmetto at home plate, they saw a flash of fire coming from the barrel of a shotgun on the porch, and they heard buckshot rattle the foliage around them. It was only after further penetrating the jungle on hands and knees that they had the glorious feeling of freedom.

After having been fortunate that the first load of buckshot missed its intended target, and knowing the low, but thick foliage they were in would ward off the force of scattered shot at that distance, the two escapees were still crawling so that no part of their bodies would be exposed.

Only a short time had passed since leaving the jail and the night was still young. Even with a full moon to bless them with its guiding power, it was only rising above the house tops and there was not light enough to assist the man with the shotgun.

The territory they had now reached seemed to have been put there to favor those who wished to keep their whereabouts a secret, but it made putting distance between them and iron jail bars much slower than these two desired, especially with their progress becoming more hampered after moving into thicker growth of the palmetto with an entanglement of vines with sharp thorns.

The men were not matched in size, and as the smaller one was being pushed ahead to break a passage through this morass of shoulder-high confusion, both kept an alert ear for sound of diamondback rattlers which they knew should be numerous in this ideal haven.

Rattlers had not been mentioned when the wily old cowhand, through his ability to set venturesome men dreaming, encouraged the men to follow this course. But there was no need for anyone in these parts to be told about the pesky critters. It was generally understood that one was safe from them only when out in a boat or in the top of a tall tree. This was not long in being discovered since the noise the men were making while on their hands and knees in total darkness awakened the snakes, and their warnings could be heard far and near.

The nerve-shattering sounds of the rattles, sometimes only a few feet away, caused the two men to debate the wisdom of continuing on or going to back to crawl through the hole in the bars of the jail cell.

In this town when someone suddenly decided to skip out for any reason, it was suspected they would ride "blind baggage" on one of the faithful freight trains which known locally as Hobo Pullmans which stopped in the town long enough to change operating crews. And so it was the next morning when the trustee came to serve the prisoners their breakfast, and found two prisoners missing and a gaping hole in the cell bars.

Other than by boat or horseback, the railroad telegraph was the only means of outside communication, and immediately after the discovery of the escape, all sheriffs in both directions along the coast were notified and asked to stop and search all freights for the escapees.

After the men left and silence settled over the jail again, the old cowhand calmly went back to sleep, to rest soundly with only the noise made by a rat chewing wood somewhere in the jail building.

Since some cowpokes were known to be experts at delivering suspicious sounding yarns of their own fabrication, the old wrangler left behind in the jail was no exception, which is why no one investigating the jail break even bothered to ask him when the men left, or took him seriously about the direction they were heading.

The little Derringer was not missed until the escapees were several miles out of town, and even then the escapees did not think the cowboy took it. The big man thought the gun had simply fallen from the secret compartment when the trousers were pulled off over his shoes while trying to get his big feet through the hole in the jail bars — and he hoped the cowboy would find and keep it for himself, before the lawmen came up to investigate.

Neither of the escapees had a gun now, and only the small one had a pocket knife, which meant their chance of obtaining food along the way was going to be pretty slim, especially since they had chosen a due west course which, if maintained without change, would be a trek of about one hundred miles of wilderness before reaching the cow town of Arcadia.

They knew where they wanted to go but had no idea of how to get there — neither the proper course to follow nor the distance to the point they wanted to reach.

But if the men had known it when leaving Fort Pierce, they could have selected a course a bit toward the southwest and found a prairie road which would have put them in the town of Tantie in less than half the distance to Arcadia. This would deliver them farther away from their crime before it was discovered. But a road, even as poor as this one, would be a prime suspected travel route, and would allow a horseman to overhaul them in short order.

After putting enough distance between themselves and the shotgun to feel out of its range, the men were now standing, but in a crouched position, and moving rapidly on into the night. Their only worries were snakes, panthers and alligators as they applied extreme effort to cover more territory before daybreak.

They had gone beyond the rough and rugged coastal fringe and were now in more open country. While they trekked steadily onward, crossing open prairies, sand ponds with gators, and various size cypress heads, they felt fresh and damp air coming at their backs. When the moon disappeared they turned to look back and saw dark rain clouds which had quickly formed over the ocean toward the east.

The fresh air they felt was off the wind which was driving the clouds toward the west. Only a short time passed before torrents of rain began pelting their backs, giving them a feeling of gratitude that now maybe their tracks and scent would be washed away.

With the fast moving cloud passing over them and going on its way to disappear somewhere in the west, the cooling rain had left them refreshed and with new energy, to cover many more miles before seeing light reflection from a rising sun in the east.

When first leaving the jail to sneak cautiously past the few residences of sleeping occupants to reach the cover of wilderness, while the ever-present chance of arousing a sleeping dog prevailed, the escapees were in a high state of anxiety and uncertainty. But as time passed so did this feeling, and now it seemed they were a sufficient distance from the sleepy little village that it may be safe to pause for a brief spell to restore their much needed energy.

Maintaining this thought while going on farther, with the sun rising at their backs, and satisfied that the rain had destroyed their back trail, they were searching for a place to hole up and rest during the day, then travel only under cover of darkness.

But before finding a suitable place for a daytime camp, and upon reaching the eastern edge of a large slough containing water and overgrown with sawgrass, their knowledge of the ways of gators created a reluctance to enter and attempt to cross, leaving them no choice but to find a way around. But in looking to the north and south for a way to bypass, there seemed to be no end.

Then, while standing at the water's edge surveying the situation, an apparent island or bayhead was seen about a quarter mile out into the body of tall grass and knee-deep water. This may be ideal. If the group of bay trees could be reached, there may be dry land and cover for a haven of a few hours.

Before reaching a decision about taking chances with battling alligators between there and the bayhead, they heard the faint sound of a flock of crows in flight at a great distance behind them. This did not demand a second thought until, after listening to it for a moment, it seemed to not be ringing true. It was taking on a different tone. Now the steady rhythm was very familiar.

Having heard the same sound before, during the period of their following the route of crime, their exchange of quick knowing glances and then the distant stare in their eyes left no doubt of their thoughts — bloodhounds were having no problem following the scent they were leaving behind, and were moving rapidly toward them.

The escapees estimated that the dogs were only a couple of miles back when first heard, so they knew the time for making plans was short. They also knew the handlers of the dogs would be on horseback which would allow the manhunt party to move much faster than the escapees had traveled for the past several miles. The situation seemed hopeless. This may very well be the end of the line.

The two men were not the only ones concerned about

the coming from the east. This dreaded sound was not a stranger to another pair of ears.

Bruce had reached the slough from the west side and gone around the north end, where he now saw the men standing at the east edge wondering if they should attempt to wade across. To capture the escapees was what Bruce was trying to do, and this chance seemed to be made to order. But now it was lost. This sound was not made by crows. There was no mistaking its source. Bruce had heard it before, and knew where there were bloodhounds on a trail there were also lawmen.

"If they recognized me when I captured them, they would certainly tell the lawmen when they reached us that I was an escapee from Raiford," Bruce was thinking to himself. Standing helpless, he watched them turn and rush back in a fast run toward the east, where they disappeared.

A short time later when the dog party reached the point on the edge of the slough where the outlaws paused while wondering about crossing the bayhead, the hounds' actions showed they, too, were acquainted with the nature of creatures of the wild. They were reluctant to enter the water registering prominently with them.

With the men's scent ending at the water's edge everyone realized they had entered at this point to wade across. Not wanting to force the dogs to follow, possibly into the jaws of sure death from alligators or cottonmouth moccasins, the two sheriff's deputies turned their mounts toward the north to take the dogs around the danger, and where they would pick up the trail on the west side of the slough.

Bruce, seeing the lawmen and dogs coming his way to go around the slough, quickly waded knee deep into

50

the water and crouched in the tall saw grass until they passed.

When finally reaching the other side and searching the area where the men would have emerged, to have the hounds fail to find scent after much coaxing, the deputies were also attracted by the body of bay trees near the center of the slough. They then knew why the dogs were not able to go any farther on the trail — the men had not come on through.

After a few minutes of visually studying the offshore island from where they were, and finding the water not deep, as they first thought, the men dismounted to wade toward the bayhead while leading the horses and walking ahead of them and the hounds.

Knowing that this great number of animals (men, horses and dogs) were creating much noise with their water splashing while crossing to the bayhead, as they came closer to find if there may be dry land, the party stopped short. While man and beast were concealed by the tall sawgrass, one of the deputies stayed with the animals and continued with the splashing of water while the other moved silently around to the other side of the growth of trees, with intentions of entering secretly and getting the drop on two surprised men who would be totally concerned with the noise the other deputy was making.

But during the time the posse of hunters were occupying themselves with improving their elaborate plan for capturing their quarry and wading to the island, the hunted men were climbing down from thickly growing boughs in the top of a large oak a half mile back the way they came where, with no time to spare, they had raced while keeping in step with their back trail, and climbed up the tree when they realized what was really making the sounds.

While sitting quietly in the treetop they had watched the dogs and riders pass directly beneath them with no let up in their pace, and without looking back, continuing until the slough stopped them. And while the lawmen were discovering there was no one but themselves on the island, the slippery escape artists were a mile beyond the south end of the slough making fast tracks toward the west.

With the greater part of the day still ahead, and having covered several miles after pulling their neat trick on the posse, the outlaws considered the distance between them and the lawmen sufficient to allow a brief period of rest, not to stop, only to reduce their pace to a walk for a spell.

Along with the aggravation of realizing that the law now knew which direction they set out in after breaking jail, hunger was becoming a physical problem. They had eaten nothing since last night in jail.

Moving steadily on their due west course, while the sun crossed the top to start its westward descent, the men had covered much more of the rough terrain and were extremely tired and hungry, but to stop for rest was out. Even though they could not hear any further sounds from the dogs after leaving the slough, those who follow this way of life know some hounds are trained to trail in silence when commanded to do so, so their quarry can be caught unaware.

Knowing hounds may be on their trail again, they changed their plans back to traveling by day instead of night. And while pushing ever onward as they kept a close watch over their back trail, watching the sun get closer and closer to the earth's western horizon, they were desperately trying for every mile possible before fatigue and hunger forced them to hole up someplace and rest.

With the sun seemingly determined to ignore them, and with many miles covered after leaving the manhunters and hounds, they reached and crossed a large and dry island of pines. Then, at a great distance ahead, a long and dark timber line could be seen stretching across their course with no end in sight in either direction.

When they finally reached the ever-increasing dark

line of timber and passed through a mile of thick forest of maple, sable palm and ancient bald cypress trees, a small and deep creek, with clear water was found winding its way to flow gently southward.

Standing motionless on the bank of the creek while watching little fishes dart here and there, the silent water and stillness of the friendly shaded forest offered a state of tranquility which had no comparison. Then, with the man-things standing immobile and the sound of their footsteps gone, birds throughout the forest could be heard again.

When recovering to awareness, the men found they were standing on a well-worn foot thoroughfare. Barefoot Indians, dogs and coons were using it regularly along with an occasional deer or turkey passing that way. Near the creek the stump of a massive ancient cypress stood, showing the tree had recently been felled. Chips were strewn along where the tree's trunk had lain, giving evidence of the recent making of an Indian long boat (dug-out or Bithlo).

Tracks of Indians pointing both directions in the soft earth of the trail indicated some type of settlement was near. A tribe, large or small, was living not far away. But just the presence of Indians was not what these renegades were afraid of. They wanted to avoid being seen by anyone who could tell the manhunters they had passed this way. And yet, Indians would have food and the two men were very much in need of it.

First seeing the forest and long before reaching it, the men thought, what we see ahead may be a blessing. It may offer a suitable place to hole up for a much needed rest and maybe we can find food while getting our bearings for the trek ahead. But with all the human sign, to stop over here would be a mistake.

Searching along the creek's bank for a way to cross, they would be off the beaten path. The outer casings from swamp cabbage were found scattered along the bank where Indians had harvested them from the tops of sable palms. One of the hearts of palm was not shelled out, but lay intact among the scattered roots removed from others. Finding the palm heart seemed a gift from above and changed their plans again. It relieved the frightful thought of having to locate the Indian tribe and the consequent risk of lying in wait until they retired to their cheekees, before they embarked on the delicate business of trying to steal food from the Indians' grub pot, which would be hanging from a long pole over the dying embers of a cook fire and which would be watched closely by hungry dogs, waiting patiently for the pot to cool.

Walking on in search of a place to cross and working on the woody cabbage with the small man's pocket knife, they removed a few of the outer roots, then began enjoying the inner tender parts on the lower end of the center casings. In order to rest a bit while further enjoying their first food since leaving the jail, they sat on the creek bank to eat most of the cabbage before realizing that any passerby would find them practically under foot.

Going on along the creek, they were not long in finding a log extending across from bank to bank where Indians had felled the tree many years earlier to create the crossing.

After serving time in prison and being taught tricks of the trade by older, long-term men, these two should have had more savvy of elusiveness, but even the best deceit artists sometime make mistakes, and so did these.

Both men were natives of south Florida and should have known that with Indians' livelihood based on their ability to hunt, they are quick to observe, and are suspicious of the sight of anything they did not create. The escapees not wanting anyone to know they had passed this way was only wishful thinking. They were doing everything short of loudly announcing their presence. Seemingly wanting to establish the fact, their first act was leaving the roots from their swamp cabbage stacked neatly where they sat to eat.

Then, if that was not enough evidence, with the little man being pushed ahead on everything as usual, he was put on the log to cross first. But the big man was not patient enough to wait for him to cross and he followed too closely. When they reached the center it was more load than the log could take.

The men were trying to keep their head above the water's surface while the remainder of their cabbage floated gently away on the current, as the knife settled into silt at the bottom.

Since the time they reached the creek, about the only thing they did that could be considered smart was, with wanting to continue on toward the west, climb from the creek on that side. They were hurrying on through the forest which bordered the creek, lest the noise of their unintentional plunge into the water may have attracted the attention of unseen but alert ears.

Passing on through the jungle growth which was not as wide as on the east, the men crossed a slight ridge of scrub oak before reaching open prairie again, exposing them to view from a great distance, and where they would have to keep a close watch on their back trail.

They would have liked very much, after crossing the creek, to stay the night in the forest on this side as planned, but after the splash-down from the broken log, staying anywhere near the creek would be unsafe.

Walking rapidly to go beyond the prairie they were

crossing while there still was light left, but with the sun now no more than a red ball about to slip below the horizon, chances of finding a secluded place to hole up seemed very remote.

Then, with the situation appearing hopeless and after going a bit farther, they could see in the blue atmospheric haze ahead, a small hammock with nothing but maybe a dozen tall sable palms growing close. This gave encouragement. The men knew that hammocks, no matter what size, only occurred where the earth was a few inches above the surrounding area. With the trunks of the trees in a tight cluster there would be no undergrowth, but dry ground.

The small body of palms seemed another blessing in the nick of time, and while trying for every drop of light from the sun, they were using all their energy to reach and then search the area for snakes before selecting a place to sleep.

But lying between them and the attractive looking hideaway was a sawgrass marsh where there would be alligators and cottonmouth moccasins. And with the marsh stretching too long in both directions across their course for them to go around and reach the hammock before night, the critters therein would simply have to bow-out from taking their toll of these two. Running as fast as the tall grass and ankle deep water would allow, they made it across, but not without wounds. The saw-edged grass did the lacerating for the snakes.

Through the marsh now, they zeroed in on the group of palms and had nearly reached them when, just ahead, they heard voices. Both men stopped and stood frozen. This was a sad moment. How had the manhunters and hounds passed to get ahead and lie in ambush? Were there no rewards for the hardships they had suffered?

It then occurred to them that even though they were listening to human voices, they were not able to understand any words being spoken. Seminole Indians talking in their language was the only answer, and with a feeling of relief the men ventured silently forward until they saw two young Indian Squaws squatted on their heels at the edge of the hammock picking small black huckleberries from low bushes.

And now with another chosen campsite suddenly becoming out of bounds, and not wanting to be seen, the men slithered away in the low prairie grass to go around the hammock hoping to find another suitable place before darkness was complete.

But they had gone only a short distance from the happy berry pickers before finding two horses nibbling the lush grass where they were left. The animals were not tethered to anything. Only short ropes were hanging from their necks with a knotted end dragging on the ground.

Even for those with several scores against them, but down on their luck, providence has no favorites. Nothing short of destiny could be responsible for this fortune.

With great enthusiasm the men moved slowly closer to grasp the ropes, then they were too close. The sudden movement to quickly grab the ropes, in itself, did not frighten the horses, and neither did the different human body odor than that of their masters, but the smell of fresh blood on the arms and faces of the men, put there by the sharp edged sawgrass, frightened and caused the horses to stand upright on their back legs while exhaling loudly with blasts of air in rapid breathing.

The horses' sudden action did not cause the men to lose their grip of the ropes, and wanting to get away quickly, each man attempted to mount. With no saddle stirrup to assist them in getting on, they were having trouble with the very nervous animals, which effort probably would have been easier if the escapees had not tried to mount from the opposite side from which the horses were accustomed. This gave the horses more evidence of dealing with strange riders and caused them to continue their bucking and loud snorting, while twisting their bodies and shaking their heads to avoid being mounted.

The escapees managed to get aboard, but hardly so before two silent figures moved simultaneously from out of nowhere with the speed of the darting shadow of a mink, to grasp a hand full of the horses' manes and in a flash, mount up in front and facing the rider of each horse.

Finding themselves lying flat on the ground at the horses' feet before hardly knowing what was happening, the thieves were no weaklings, but knew the surprise element was what swung the pendulum in favor of the two young Seminole Braves who had been hunting bullfrogs in the nearby marsh while the Squaws picked berries.

With a coil of rope which one of the Braves had hanging from his waist, and while loud accusations of horse stealing were voiced in broken English by both the Indians, a loop was fashioned around the neck of the large escapee. His hands were tied together at the wrists with a strong rawhide throng, before the horse was urged forward forcing the man to follow at the end of the rope.

Darkness was now about complete. While the horse was gradually made to walk faster, with the big outlaw stumbling along, loud protests came while he tried to stay on his feet so that his neck would not be stretched. While keeping his horse close behind the man at the end of the rope, the other Indian was urging the necktie party along.

Fully expecting the end to come when a tree was

found with limbs stout enough to support the weight of his body, the large man's mind was racing for some avenue of escape. But with no trees on the prairie other than sable palms with no limbs, and tall pines with limbs too high to reach, the party kept moving while the horse was coaxed into even greater speed.

No one could last long with this punishment. After a short period of stumbling while running as fast as he could, the Indians saw their prisoner was not able to gain his feet anymore. Exhaustion had robbed his strength and he now lay dragging on his stomach.

Feeling the weight on his rope and looking back, the Brave on the lead horse knew that with the choking action of the rope the man would only survive a very

short time. He drove his horse on a bit farther before stopping to dismount and to find the condition of the body to his satisfaction. Retrieving the rope, both horsemen galloped rapidly back to rope the small horse thief and give him the same treatment.

But the Braves, as smart as Indians are, never before had the pleasure of reckoning with the wiliness of seasoned tricksters such as these two.

Tying the man's hands together in front of his body instead of behind allowed him the freedom of using both hands together and grasp the rope to pull slack and take the pressure off his neck. And Indian mistake number two: They should have examined the body more closely. This outlaw was an expert at playing dead when the advantage was to do so.

The small outlaw saw there was only one rope and estimated what to expect after they finished off his partner. He did not come into view, neither did he stay back where the "party" started, where the Braves expected to find him waiting. Immediately after the two Indians turned their mounts to go back for the little man, he crept out of the darkness to kneel beside the limp body of his buddy.

Finding him apparently dead but maybe with enough spark to be revived, the little man started moving all limbs and mashing and rubbing the big man's stomach hoping he would start breathing. But at that moment the man raised to sit up. There was no reviving necessary. Only an idiot would continue fighting a hopeless battle, particularly when perfect timed deceit would make the day.

Moving quickly to another place when they heard the Indians coming back after they did not find the little man where they left him, the two escapees waited from where they were concealed in total darkness, until the sounds of the horses disappeared, as the Braves headed west in search of both men after finding the big one also gone.

That the Indians noticed the carefully placed outer sections of their swamp cabbage on the bank of the creek was not known by the escapees to have aroused suspicion with the first Indians to pass that way, or else they would not have felt so safe after the horse-riding Braves rose on west in search of them.

It was not until late that night when other Indians, while following the trail along the creek, noticed the cabbage refuse and suddenly became alert to strangers passing that way. Knowing that only white men would leave their trash in that condition, they wanted to know why they were in Cow Creek territory.

Two young Braves were appointed to investigate. In darkness they followed the creek until they found the broken foot crossing, where they crossed in the water to follow the route of the two white men, continuing on until crossing the marsh and reaching the small palm hammock.

Upon finding vegetation disturbed at the edge of the hammock, they felt the ground in darkness to find sign where the same two men with shoes had been there. Expecting the men to be in the hammock asleep, they began making plans. Upon further examination of the ground surface they found barefoot Indians and horses had created quite a commotion near the hammock.

Knowing the two horseback Braves and their Squaws were in the area frog hunting and berry picking, and with now finding sign which could have been made by none other than them, these two Indian Braves were satisfied the situation had been taken care of properly.

Just short of entering the thick palm hammock, the

two investigating Braves turned and went back to the creek and their tribe, where they knew the frog hunters would now have the attentive ear of all the other members while telling of their interesting experience about routing the white men from their hunting grounds.

The following morning with light rays high in the eastern sky, the two men crept stealthily from where they had holed up in the only safe place in the surrounding area, where their whereabouts would not be suspected — in the little palm hammock where they had planned to stay in the first place.

The two escapees were cunning and had outsmarted the Indians, but they were not the only ones who knew where they had holed up. Bruce had witnessed their every move since gaining sight of them again at the sawgrass slough. Again he could have captured the men at this point but he thought to himself, "They are heading in the direction which I would take them as prisoners. Why should I have to prevent their escaping from me the entire way? Let them get closer to the jail before I take them."

As the sun rose above the treetops toward the east, the two would-be just-disappointed horse thieves were several miles to the west of where they camped.

The jail breakers were somewhat rested from the long trek of yesterday, but with having no food other than the swamp cabbage, they were much weaker and knew they would not be able to go far today without finding something which would sustain their minds and bodies.

With heat of the day developing rapidly as the two men trudged on and on, they could see small open prairie areas ahead, and when reaching each of them, which were no more than a few acres, they increased their pace to cross quickly while under constant fear of their exposure attracting the Indians again, leaving them no possible chance of escaping the fast horsemen.

Yesterday had been long, with hard traveling and stressful events, and they were forced to go farther than they wished. They had no intentions of repeating those experiences today.

This day, with so great a need for food, but with no firearm nor fishing tackle, they would spend more time along the way searching for something that could be obtained without either. Anything — wild fruits, berries or maybe another discarded swamp cabbage.

Along with secretly packing the hacksaw blade, they wished they had thought to include a fish hook and line with their emergency equipment, because then they could have perch or bass from some of the many ponds they were passing. "Or maybe farther on there will be a bird's nest with eggs," they thought.

With the sun at their backs casting their shadow ever shorter before them, the men were slowing moving westward from one thickly-forested palm and oak hammock, across open prairies and sand ponds, to others, while searching each at length for some form of food, but in vain. Even the small bullfrogs found along the edge of sand ponds were too fast for them.

Moving perpetually onward with the day seeming to be moving slower than yesterday, as hunger became more intense, the men began to wonder if lack of food may affect their minds, causing them to move only in circles over a wide area in this wild and remote area until they perished. As time passed this thought grew increasingly stronger until, with the last spark of reasoning the small outlaw possessed, he realized their continuing in this manner would only increase the possibility and grasped the big man's arm while saying to him, "I can go no farther. Let's stop and rest!"

Sitting silently on a decaying log at the outer edge of another and somewhat larger hammock, where the remaining strength in their half-starved bodies had lent itself toward restoring their failing brains, faintly, at a considerable distance, they heard the sound of crows again.

Unlike yesterday, when now hearing the dreaded sound, they knew what it was. Lacking the energy they had then, this time they would not be able to employ the same tactics. Instead of quickly backtracking as they did then, to climb a tree and confuse the dogs, they would have to move on as fast as possible and hope for the best.

Moving with fright of what might happen when the dogs reached them, and with a bit more energy after the brief rest, they struggled to push their way through the thicker growth of foliage on the fringe of the hammock to gain clear open space which they knew would be in the shadows of tall palms and spreading branches of the large oaks, feeling that they could move faster and maybe leave the hounds.

As they broke through to the less congested area, the alarming sound came to them again, but this time they were able to place it dead ahead instead of on their back trail as they first thought.

Slowing their pace and venturing cautiously, they had gone deeper into the shadows of the trees to where the sound was now growing clearer, where it could be determined that it was indeed a flock of crows under stress of some disturbance, instead of the voice of blood-hounds.

With the relief this brought, the men were ready to stop again for a longer period of rest. Sitting on a large protruding root and leaning against the trunk of a mighty oak, they realized after only a few moments that the rapid "caw-cawing" was coming east toward them.

With it definitely established that the crows were coming their way, if whatever it was did not change course, the cause of the crows' noise would reach the oak the men were sitting under in a very short time. The men were weary of what might be the cause of this commotion with the birds. With no protection, not even a pocket knife after yesterday, they wanted to prevent being caught short if more Indians were headed toward them.

Well in advance of the sound of the noisy birds reaching them, the fugitives shifted position to a small nearby cluster of lower growth foliage which would conceal them. They sat on the ground and waited as the "cawing" sound gradually came closer.

But the waiting in ambush did not last long before they heard grunting on the ground, with the crows flying directly above. Then they heard lighter sounding grunts and short little squeals before a family of wild hogs came into view a short distance away.

A large black boar, with sharp four-inch long tusks projecting from the sides of its snout bending upward at the ends, was leading, followed by a long razorback mama hog, with her flock of ten-pound, fat and playful pigs. The two older hogs were searching the leaves under the oaks with their snouts for fallen acorns.

Watching with interest from their hidden position only a few yards away, the escapees could see the beasts knew nothing of their presence, and were thoroughly enjoying the crunchy morsels they were finding.

But these men knew nothing about the nature of hogs, especially wild ones. They had no gun nor knife. Neither had they ever eaten roast pig, but they did have matches and there was firewood.

Waiting patiently, with their hunger growing more

intense, the men watched the unsuspecting animals move slowly on past them before silently, and with the speed of a mink, positioning themselves behind a large oak just ahead of where the pigs were playing.

When the small playful animals reached the tree, one of them scampered around it while asking to be chased, but it failed to get all the way around the tree. The squeal of a pig at play is different from when in distress. The speed of electricity is slow when compared to the time it took the adult boar to reach the tree.

As one escapee quickly dropped the pig and reached for a limb, the boar already had a large bite of the big man's pants. As the man reached for the next limb up, to see the little man already three limbs higher, the boar was trying for something more than pants.

Pulling himself up to escape the sharp teeth only by the thickness of his shorts, he left the enraged boar with its front feet now resting against the trunk of the tree while standing on its back ones and jumping, hoping for one more bite of the enemy.

Sitting much higher up and safely out of reach of the vicious and lightening fast varmint, the men had temporarily forgotten food. Their only concern now was for the hogs to move on their way with their acorn hunting, so that the men could come down from the tree and continue on their own way.

If the men had entertained any doubt of the course they were following being the right one, there surely was none now. This course that, seemingly some mysterious force caused them to select when leaving Fort Pierce and which they had followed to this point, could be none other than the "Wild Boar Trail."

But this large and dark hammock had more acorns to offer than most others and was the favorite feeding

ground for this family. They had no intentions of hurrying away just to accommodate a proven enemy — up a
tree or not.

Before having the run-in with the boar the sun was
already over the top and was now drifting slowly westward while the men in the tree fretted, and the hogs on
the ground under them calmly rooted out more acorns.

This situation was becoming very undesirable. The
small man was thinking, "Here we perch on a limb watching sure death below, all because some stupid wild animals considered a few acorns more important than the
life of two honest, but totally helpless men."

While the sun was now almost touching the treetops,

68

and their hopes of ever getting to leave the safety of their tree about gone, the feeding animals drifted slowly on toward the east about as unconcerned as they were when they came, while Bruce enjoyed the show from a concealed place in a nearby tree.

Watching the hogs drift on away from the tree, and when thinking it may be safe, the men silently climbed down on the opposite side and moved with the speed of a frightened jacksnipe, while keeping the thick trunk of the tree between themselves and that large ball of anger, and they constantly watched over their shoulders.

Chances of finding food now before night were about nil. Even if some possibility for food occurred, which would have interested them earlier, there would be no time before night to investigate. With the hogs not far behind, who knew when they would decide they had enough acorns for one day and might come back this way.

Going on as rapidly as they were able and as long as they dared before stopping for the night, they had reached another small palm hammock. The place was not at all attractive. There was nothing but tall skinny sable palms with needle sharp spines the entire length of their trunks. There were no trees with limbs. But darkness was closing in. This place would simply have to do. They would take turns, with one sleeping while the other stood watch. Then they remembered that fire will ward off certain animals. Maybe this boar was one of them.

Feeling around on the ground with their hands in the darkness, they collected enough dry palm frond stems to get a bright fire going. Heavier wood was found to make the fire more permanent. Then both men curled up on the west side of the fire and quickly fell asleep.

They did not encounter any problems during their hungry, fitful rest, wild boars or otherwise. Even though the lack of food for so long had left them almost too weak to walk any farther, they were moving slowly westward again when the sun gave its first reflection of light high in the eastern sky, announcing the coming of another day.

Covering several more miles after leaving the little hammock where they camped, and now with the sun up to a mid-morning position, the slow moving man-things had disturbed many wild creatures, some of which could have been the makings of a fine dinner, only to watch them run or fly away.

Not far ahead, a long thin strand of young pointed top cypress trees was seen stretching across their course. When they reached the point to cross the narrow strip, they found themselves suddenly against a two-rutted prairie road.

Finding the road so abruptly after covering the vast wilderness since breaking jail was no less than frightening. Civilization was the last thing they wanted. But then, they thought, an area with a road to travel also had people to travel it, and where there were people there was food.

Standing beside the road wondering what move to make and which way to go, they heard sounds coming from the north. Then a thin, long legged horse pulling a light buckboard wagon, with one man sitting where he had the seat placed at the front of the wagon body, was rapidly coming toward them, headed south. The horse was in a fast, long stepping trot while the man leaned forward, as if he thought this position would cut down on wind resistance and assist the horse with pulling the wagon.

Wanting to avoid contact with anyone until they could survey the situation a bit further, the men quickly stepped backward into the thick growth of young trees they had just emerged from. They watched the wagon come and pass along the road only a few feet from where they were hidden, then saw "US MAIL" painted on the back. The daily mail run between Fort Drum and Tantie was late and the driver was trying to recover the loss and arrive in Tantie on schedule.

When the fast wagon rounded a curve in the sandy two rutted road and disappeared from their view, the escapees came from cover to stand in the road while planning their next move.

They knew they would not be able to go far this day without food. And knowing now that mail was being transported between two points, where either point would have residents and food stores, and very likely some type of lawman, they considered briefly what to do. With hunger dominating their every thought, they would simply have to take a chance, and seemingly the most logical thing for them to do was to follow the wagon.

CHAPTER 5

Having followed the men this great distance since their break from the Fort Pierce jail, Bruce was pleased when they began following the prairie road. He was now back in familiar territory, and knew where the road led to, and knew the tough Sheriff in Tantie had a reputation of investigating all strangers.

Bruce was certain that when the men reached Tantie they would be captured and returned to prison, relieving him of the possibility of their exposing him as an escapee from Raiford. He could now go back to his fishing at Buckhead Ridge.

Walking as briskly as hunger and weakness would allow, the escapees covered only a few miles along the road before they reached another but lesser dirt road. This road was more crooked where it turned here and there to go between and around trees. Looking to the west, along the course of the road, they could see a house a half mile away.

Following the crooked road toward the place, they passed a field of shoulder-high corn. Then they were nearer and could see the house was made of logs. There was a barn and two smaller buildings, all constructed of rough-sawed pine boards, with none ever having the benefit of paint.

Getting closer, a briar berry patch lay hard against one side of the road, with the thick and thorny briar bushes about waist high and loaded with luscious ripe blackberries, making temptation too great for the men to resist.

Both men waded into the briar patch with the big one leading this time, instead of pushing the little man first as he did in all other questionable areas. They were picking and eating the berries with both hands, with the big man leading farther into the patch while the little one, having moved back a bit, was contented with those he could reach from where he stood at the edge of the road.

They were thoroughly enjoying the berries, their first food since the swamp cabbage two days ago back at Cypress Creek, but had not been in the patch long enough to satisfy their hunger before a blood-curdling scream came from the big man. Then he staggered to the road dragging a large rattler with its fangs hooked into his leg below the knee.

The big man was frightened to a state of helplessness. All he was able to do was yell and his buddy kicked the snake's head loose from its grip and he pulled the man out of the snake's reach. They both were now yelling for help, but from whom they did not know.

While having no thought of anyone being within miles of their place, the homesteader and his wife were having their noon day lunch when they heard the screaming and calls for help. When they recognized the fact that the commotion was coming from the berry patch, they knew just what had happened.

Toppling his chair over from his quick movement to

get away from the table, the farmer raced toward the door while yelling back to his wife, "Grab the rope and come on. Old Snag-Fang has got him another one!"

His sharp pocket knife was open and ready when the farmer reached the scene to find the victim sitting on the ground swaying back and forth, trying to rub the venom back down and out of his leg at the wound, moaning for help before he died.

The little man had already removed his own belt and had it drawn tight around the leg just above the knee.

When the farmer squatted beside the victim to inspect the two long and bleeding fang marks, which had begun to swell, he immediately made a few cuts in the same area with the sharp knife, then put his mouth over the entire works and began pulling blood from it.

Upon arriving, the farmer's wife quickly twisted the rope tourniquet on the leg and removed the temporary and useless belt which the small man had applied, while he moved about wanting to help with something, anything.

After pulling enough blood from the wound that the homesteader felt he had removed all the venom, they lifted the man to his feet and walked him to the house where the rope was removed to let the blood circulate through the leg and bleed freely from the wound for a bit to additionally cleanse the operation.

The patient then was seated in a rocker on the porch where he now felt he might now have a new lease on life. The farmer's wife bathed the wound and applied medication and a dressing, before going into the kitchen to prepare more food so that the two strangers could dine with them.

When the food was ready the snake-bit man was able to move into the dining room under his own power, where he and his partner ate ravenously, while listening to the history of the big rattlesnake.

They were told the snake was here when the family settled on their homestead ten years ago, and was seen several times during each summer but it managed to elude all attempts to destroy it. It had fanged two other people in the briar patch, with the last one just a week ago when a traveling peddler also was not able to resist the sparkling black delicacies. The rope was prepared then, and kept for those who may follow.

Old "Snag Fang," they were told, was given this name by the farmer after the fang marks it left on the first victim. The gash left by one of the fangs was not as deep or as long as the other, indicating one of the snake's weapons was broken, with about half of it missing.

Having managed to exchange their prison stripes for civilian wear at a family clothes line shortly after leaving the state prison, which allowed them to go in and out of jail at Fort Pierce without being suspected as escapees, they were now enjoying the same freedom. With the appearance of nothing more than two drifters who were down on their luck, they were treated like royalty.

Only the heavy prison issue shoes they both wore offered any indication of their identity, but these farm folks knew nothing about prison shoes, and the fact that both men were wearing the same brand and color rang no bell with them, as it did not with the Sheriff at the Fort Pierce jail.

Learning from their benefactors that the mail wagon was following a road leading to Tantie, which connected with another that would allow them to reach the west coast of the State. The escapees thought, "And if we follow the road the opposite way, it will take us to where we broke jail if we want to go back. Not likely!"

After having the hearty noonday meal with the home-steaders the "drifters" wanted to leave without delay, but yielded when the farmer and his wife suggested staying overnight to allow the wound more time for recovery before subjecting the leg to another stretch of hard walking.

Farm work is never quite finished. And with the project of this day not completed before their guests arrived, and which could not be put off until another day, the farmer went back to it after lunch, leaving the two strangers enjoying the cool of the porch shade while his wife went about her housework.

With their closest neighbors either in Fort Drum or Tantie, and each several miles from the farm, these folks were starved for someone to talk to, and after more fine food for supper, all four sat in the cool night air on the porch where the farmer and his wife unsuspectingly exposed their fortunes and misfortunes to the two "honest but unfortunate strangers."

Hospitality was not lacking for these two. The spare bedroom was made comfortable for them, and while they rested peacefully on the bed of a free man for the first time since leaving home to enter prison to serve their long sentence, the homesteader's wife busied herself with patching the big man's trousers where the wild boar missed his point.

When morning came and they had indulged further into the graces of good hosts, to the extent where they felt they could now walk a hundred miles without another bite of food, no amount of coaxing would keep them any longer.

The friendly treatment and wanting them to hang around longer seemed too good. Who knew if there were a phone hidden someplace and connected with that tough law man in Fort Pierce who invited them ever so politely to "Draw, you polecats, if you think you are fast! But in case you are not so sure, then come on out of that freight car gentle like and get ahead of me cause we're going to march to the jail!"

After having breakfast, with signs of day showing in the east, the three men sat for a moment on the porch where they all rolled cigarettes from the farmer's sack of tobacco. Then, with the time of departure near, the big man excused himself and went for a moment back through the dark living room to their bedroom. He came back to the porch and without tarrying announced to their host that they would be on their way. The farmer walked with them to the yard gate, then waved farewell as the two men disappeared in the morning mist.

With not missing his sack of tobacco until reaching his work, the farmer laid it to forgetfulness and worked all forenoon without a smoke. It was not until he and his wife came from the field at noon, where they had worked hard trying to accomplish what was neglected because of their guests, that they were shocked beyond words at finding the large revolver gone from its regular place on the mantle over the fireplace.

Only a glance was necessary now to confirm the sudden thoughts of both. The money, too, was gone from the china bud vase which always sat on top of the fold-down sewing machine. Eleven dollars of hard-earned money, saved over the entire year to pay taxes in the fall. Only a few coins were left — coins which would have rattled if removed from the vase to place into a pocket.

There would be no going back to work in the fields this day. The farmer stood against the mantle while his wife sat on the edge of a chair, both in silence with their minds racing for an answer. They could hardly believe it. The men were so friendly and smart. They seemed to have the right answers for everything. But still, there was no one else around who could have taken the gun and money.

The thieves had left them with two guns but both were shotguns. Even though they would be fast and accurate, they did not have the range of the big revolver removed from the mantle.

Half a day had passed since their friendly guests departed, and if they expected to be followed after their crime was discovered, there was little hope of the farmer overtaking them on foot. His only other means of transportation was with his yoke of oxen. One of them was broken to saddle. He could ride it but it was the older one and had pulled the plow all morning and would be too tired to do anything more than walk slowly.

Not waiting for lunch, he hitched the younger ox to the small, light wagon and with one of the two shotguns he brought loaded with buckshot, he and his wife boarded quickly to rush to the main road hoping the mail wagon had not passed on its way to Tantie.

Their wait at the road was not long. After explaining the situation to the mail carrier, the farmer boarded the buckboard with the gun, leaving his wife to follow in the ox wagon with the other shotgun, and meet him in Tantie.

Fully expecting the fast mail wagon to overhaul the men before reaching Tantie, the farmer's plans were, when seeing the men in the road ahead, to lie flat on the wagon floor until they were abreast of the thieves. If only the mail carrier were seen in the wagon, the men would not become suspicious and run into the woods to escape. They would only step aside and let the wagon pass, giving closer range for the shotgun, if it was pressed into service.

It was thought that when the men were captured, they would be hauled into Tantie and turned over to the Sheriff, with the farmer waiting there for the arrival of his wife in the slow moving ox wagon so that they would have transportation back to their homestead.

Even though the mail horse was fast, they completed the long trip to Tantie without finding any sign of the men.

Not finding them along the way was an alarming experience for the homesteader. He knew they could not have reached town ahead of the buckboard, especially with one of them limping along on a lame leg. Maybe they had stopped some place to rest.

The farmer explained everything to the Sheriff as quickly as possible before he headed back toward home in a fast run, hoping to meet the ox wagon about half way. After running fast as long as he was able, he then jogged for awhile, only to finally reduce this to fast walking. Then hardly able to put one foot ahead of the other, he reached the half-way point, but there was no ox wagon.

Knowing the wagon certainly should have reached here by now, he was more distressed but too tired to go farther. Forcing his body to generate a bit more energy, he had gone only a few more steps when he found sign in the sandy road where the wagon turned off the road and had gone toward the west. Closer inspection showed foot prints of men where the wagon stopped before leaving the road.

Frustration ran high with the farmer when the mail wagon reached Tantie with no sign of the thieves along the way, but that was nothing compared with his thoughts now. He knew the marks in the road were put there only a short time before his arrival, and the slow wagon could not have gone far.

Following the wagon sign as fast as his ebbing strength and the rough terrain would allow, he went deep into the pine forest before reaching an area with course grass which would spring back up when stepped on, leaving no sign made by wagon wheels nor the hooves of the ox. And after spending considerable time searching a wide area for further sign, but unsuccessfully, there was only one thing left to do — go back to Tantie for a saddle horse and bloodhounds.

Following the wagon sign into the woods showed that the course it was taking was slightly toward the southwest which, if continued in that direction, would reach the Kissimmee River not far upstream from where it enters the lake.

Hours later when the farmer staggered back into the Sheriff's office to report the latest findings, word was not long in spreading through the neighborhood, and forty to fifty horsemen with all colors and brands of dogs following, quickly assembled at the Sheriff's office.

It was decided that with the wagon taking a southwest course, if it did not change, it could be cut off before reaching the river, causing the impatient posse to quickly gallop off on a northwest course.

With man and beast rallying to the cause, they made a whirlwind departure into a wilderness they all knew well.

Their calculations were accurate except for timing. It was a bit off. The hounds picked up scent where the wagon crossed their course only a short time before. Changing their northwest course to follow the dogs, they were not long in reaching the river, only to find a nearly exhausted ox hitched to the wagon and standing at the water's edge, but no sign of the homesteader's wife or the thieves.

Many catfishermen's wives help with the family trotlines. So when a lake fishing boat with its traditional high bow, carrying two men and a woman, was seen at daybreak entering the lake from the Kissimmee River, heading toward where Bruce and his two Indian fishing partners were in the lake offshore from the tribe's camp on Buckhead Ridge working with their trotlines, it was given no particular thought until the boat came close to pass them.

Many years had passed since Bruce first saw these two men in prison. Even then his association with them was brief, with them in his sight so many times after their jail break in Fort Pierce, there was no chance of mistaken identity. He left them in Raiford doing time for getting caught selling the colorful shells of tree snails to shell collectors.

But Bruce did not dare make contact with them now because he knew their caliber. They would remember that when he left the chain gang he gave back to the State eleven months of his one-year sentence, and they just might be in need of the one hundred dollar reward on his head. But he could be mistaken about their identity. The common lake fishing boat they were in, and the woman, just didn't add up to law breakers.

With Bruce's deeply tanned face and the Seminole Indian shirt he was wearing, the men in the motorboat paid him no mind. They thought he was just another Indian. But when their boat was abreast of the rowboat, the woman's actions were noticeable. They were not at all normal. She appeared very nervous, and seemed to be trying to convey some message with her hands. But when the motorboat passed on along the shore line toward the west, nothing more was thought of it.

After reaching the river to find nothing but the ox and wagon, the posse was temporarily at a dead end. After searching the bank of the river for a considerable distance in both directions, to see nothing but fishermen's shanties and with no one having seen any strangers, some members of the posse acquired a boat and crossed to search the other side, in the event the trio swam the river.

After leaving the rig at the river bank, it was as if the three people went straight up. No sign of any kind was found by the posse, on land or water.

Then, thinking the thieves and their captive may have tried to distract anyone who may follow, the pursuers wondered if the trio had left a moving wagon just short of the river and walked away from where they knew a tracker could follow sign.

This thought brought the dogs back into service. They were led slowly in ever widening semi-circles, from river around the wagon and to river again. But these dogs were not trained for the purpose. They were only hunting dogs, watch dogs and just plain dogs. Only a few of them paid any attention to human scent.

Continuing to enlarge the search area, and to question again and more extensively every member of the fishing families living along the river, the pursuers carried on throughout the night. When day arrived and a fisherman's motorboat was missing, the search took on new dimensions. Faster motorboats were pressed into service to search the river, both north and south.

Knowing the fishing boat was slow, it was expected that the fast boats would catch it before going far on the river. But on second thought, if the fishing boat were acquired by the fugitives soon after leaving the wagon, they had been on the water all night and could be a long way from there.

The search boat working down the river toward the lake reached the open water with no success. It then turned toward the east and searched the shoreline of Eagle Bay before following the lakeshore around to the mouth of Taylor Creek.

Still with no success, the day was spent with everyone in the search party offering his theory of where to find the missing trio, while the fast boats were scouring the water's edge but seemingly to always be going in the wrong direction. None were searching the lake toward the west.

After another night passed while the search continued. The organized effort had about given way to everyone searching alone, and in his own way.

When Toby and Louis, the Seminole Braves who were Bruce's fishing partners, met him at their dock at daybreak, to go into the lake and harvest the night's catch of catfish, there was no boat to use for the purpose. Bruce's rowboat was gone and a lake-style motorboat was hard aground a few feet short of the dock.

As all three men recognized the boat from yesterday, they knew its presence could mean only one thing — the two boats were switched during the night. But why? Was the boat out of fuel, or had the engine failed for some other reason?

The motorboat's presence put Bruce to wondering if the two men they saw in the boat with the woman really were who he first thought them to be. Was the motorboat "hot" and they wanted to ditch it to lessen the chance of their getting caught? But if they wanted to get away fast, why take a rowboat? Why his rowboat?

Bruce found this most confusing. It was the second time his little rowboat had been taken by thieves. Before it had gotten him involved with egret plume poachers and the Audubon Society, which nearly cost him his freedom. And this time he hoped to avoid such a chapter. But one thing was for sure — his boat was gone again without his permission. This was an insult. It was more than he cared to tolerate, and if the boat was not destroyed, he would find it.

He knew what the men were serving time in prison for and suspected they were headed back to start again. With the easy money to be made in the tree snail business, it was very tempting, even for semi-honest souls.

If the boats were switched early last night the thieves would have several hours head start on him. Even with the slow rowboat which, if the woman was still with them, would be loaded to its capacity, they still could have traveled far from Buckhead Ridge. There could be no delay in getting started to camping on their trail.

Knowing the fishermen could use the heavy Indian dugout boat for tending their lines, Bruce told his partners he knew where his boat was going, and he would leave on foot immediately to follow the west shoreline around the lake and try to head them off before they reached their destination, maybe at Lakeport, or at least before they passed Moore Haven.

Hurrying to his cheekee, he conversed briefly with his wife, Fannie, before touching Tag, his dog and Varmint, the pet coon, and grabbing a handful of food which could be eaten on the run. Bruce then disappeared over the ridge among elderberry bushes and popash trees, heading southwest in a steady run.

He had been gone only a short time when one of the search boats passed where the two Braves were at the dock working on their fishing equipment. The boat turned after going a bit farther and came back to the dock and stopped next to them.

The men in the search boat saw the motorboat near the dock, and with it being exactly like many others around the lake, thought it belonged to the Indians. They had come back to tell the Braves they were searching for two men and a woman in a boat like theirs, but the Indians were quick to inform the search party that the boat did not belong to their tribe.

They then told the searchers everything they knew about the boat: when they first saw it, who was in it, when it arrived at their dock and about Bruce's rowboat being gone. When told Bruce was gone in search of his boat, the men immediately wanted to know where Bruce expected to find the boat. But Bruce had not told them where he was going to look for the boat, so they were not able to help. In their effort to explain, they aroused suspicion. Being fishing partners and not knowing where he was going, was hard for the searchers to believe. But then, when finding there was nothing more to learn from the Indians, the men in the search boat took the stolen one in tow and headed up the Kissimmee to the owner for him to identify.

Bruce's endurance was strong this day and, even with having to wade much prairie water and push through many thick growths of popash and elderberry covered with an entanglement of moonvine, not to mention crossing sawgrass sloughs infested with gators and moccasins, he was making very good time and had covered many miles when the sun had reached its summit.

CHAPTER 6

Their long prison stretch was not done with the escapees learning nothing. They were cunning enough to know if a party of two men and a woman were seen rowing along leisurely in a small boat they would cause no suspicion, and they were in no hurry. And, too, the owner of a rowboat would not be as likely to report it stolen as would the owner of a motorboat. But these two thieves had not studied their lesson very well. They had not learned the nature of one Bruce Coggins.

While cruising in choppy water with a constant southeast breeze against it, the rowboat was not traveling as fast as Bruce was on land, but it had a long head start on him and when reaching Compton's store in Lakeport, with the sun now about down, Bruce found that the boat arrived in Lakeport about mid-morning, where one of the men occupants came into the store and bought food before pushing off hurriedly to be on their way toward Moore Haven.

Learning this, Bruce was now more sure of where the men were heading. And with that thought, there was no sense in pushing on into the night where he would be taking a chance with rattlers. He would simply follow them to their destination, no matter how far behind. He asked and received permission from Compton to sleep on the porch of the store that night.

Bruce also bought food before the store closed for the night, and was on his way again when the morning light was sufficient for him to travel safely. He started out walking, then this developed into a jog and finally, after warming up, into his regular long stepping run, which put him in Moore Haven with much of the forenoon to spare.

When reaching the town, he noted a paddle-wheel steamboat was moored along the bank of the river near the lone cypress tree which served as a guiding beacon for all craft crossing the large lake. Black smoke was belching from the steamer's tall stack, where the fireman was poking fat pine into the firebox, making ready for the departure.

Old and with a long gray beard, the Captain of the ship stood on shore where he was announcing that, "This ship will leave in ten minutes for La Belle and points beyond. All passengers going that way, put your baggage on board now! There will be no delay! When the whistle blows all lines will be cast off!"

Hearing this and knowing he could do a lot in ten minutes, Bruce dashed into Parkinson's general store to inquire if anyone had seen the rowboat pass through. He was told by the owner of store that the trio was in his store late in the afternoon yesterday, where they made a few purchases before pushing off down the Caloosahatchee toward La Belle, "and with the two men laughing at that crazy woman they had with them, for the silly motions she was making with her hands!"

While standing against the rail waiting for the whistle to announce the ship's departure, Bruce thought, "Maybe with leaving Moore Haven so late in the day, the men planned to camp for the night along the river, which would cut their lead over him down by ten to twelve hours. And maybe the steamboat would overhaul them before they made it all the way through the river to Fort Myers!" Then the whistle blew and the feel of the boat's movement away from the river bank was noticeable when the blades of the big waterwheel started taking deep bites in the water.

Assisted by the current of the water, the big boat was cruising much faster than Bruce could on foot, putting him at ease and happy with the progress. But he knew the thieves also would have benefit of the fast outgoing water. If they did not stop and camp, he suspected they would be in Fort Myers by this time.

As the ship moved swiftly along, with many possibilities coming to mind, he let no objects pass unseen, in the event the rowboat was delayed along the way and passed before the steamer reached its destination.

After a short delay in La Belle to accommodate passengers, take care of the freight business and pick up a supply of fat pine wood for the boiler, the boat continued on its way south to reach the broader waters near Fort Myers when the sun was setting.

Light was falling fast when the boat tied up at the town dock, where the Captain announced this was the end of the run. "This ship will lay over here tonight and leave at daybreak for the return trip, where it will cruise the east side of the lake this time, and go all the way to the town of Kissimmee, stopping at all points between!"

Before his feet were barely on the ground, Bruce saw his boat. The bow was pulled up on shore at the land end of the dock. With darkness nearly complete, making visibility poor, he went directly to the boat to make sure it was not one similar to his. He did not have to touch the boat to know he was right. Stepping in to walk to the stern and check it out, he found a shotgun with its stock resting on the floor and the barrel leaning against a seat. With no one noticing, he could have pushed the boat off and been on his way, but Bruce did not do business this way. It was not his style to run out on a job half finished when there was a debt to pay, especially when it involved his property.

He guessed the thieves were not far away and would be coming back soon to the boat, else they would not have left the gun. He planned to conceal himself under the dock and await their return. But no part of his plan was carried out. Before leaving the boat he saw the batwing doors of a saloon across the dirt street from the waterfront burst open and out ran the two thieves, while pushing the woman ahead of them, and with the saloon keeper in hot pursuit behind them.

Running while trying to aim, the bartender was pouring lead at the trio, but with no accuracy. His aim was poor enough even while standing and his target was not stopping any of the bullets. But Bruce almost did. He was in direct line behind them and dropped to the floor of the boat when hearing the first bullet zip past. With the boat having very low sides he was still having to do some fast dodging.

Running ahead of the men, the woman reached the boat first, where, without noticing Bruce, she grabbed the shotgun and turned back toward the firing line.

Bruce saw her reaching for the gun but was not fast enough. He knew her intentions and rushed forward before she could use it on the saloon man. Jumping off the bow of the boat to catch her, he kicked the gun from her hands, then raked it into the water with his foot.

Pushing their "gun moll" ahead of him so that he could use her for a shield and have all three in view, Bruce ordered the small man, who was closer and had no gun, to raise his hands. When hearing this the barkeep knew he had an ally, and held his fire.

The big thief who had the revolver but could not do much shooting behind him while running, also heard Bruce's order and knew he now had another enemy.

Ignoring the bartender who couldn't shoot straight

anyway, the big thief turned quickly to face Bruce intending to exchange fire with him. The big fellow's intentions were fast enough but his trigger finger did not cooperate and there was only one shot fired.

While calmly placing the little thirty-two caliber hammerless Owls Head revolver back into his side pocket, Bruce covered the short space to reach the man and pick up the heavy revolver which had been shot from his

hand, and which was now lying at his feet with the larger man looking longingly at it while rubbing his numb fingers.

Rapid gunfire on the waterfront was not long in attracting company. The Sheriff with two of his deputies, and a policeman, the entire police force, with drawn guns were closing in on all sides. Beams from their flashlights caught the group in the dirt street about half way between the saloon and the water. Seeing the bartender with his white apron, the lawmen knew where the trouble started, and they proceeded to take charge.

Seeing the woman in the group, the officers knew this was, as usual, just another barroom brawl, started with two drunks over a skirt. But before any of the lawmen's questions could be answered, the woman rushed forward to hastily butt in with her explanation. With rapid-fire speech she told of her abduction by these two men, and being held prisoner under threat of death if she tried to escape or communicate with anyone.

Her fast cock-and-bull story sounded too fantastic to be true, and the lawmen took it to be just another familiar attempt to stay out of jail by trying to implicate someone else in a more serious crime. The officers were about ready to discount the woman's entire story and put all four, including Bruce, in jail. They thought all present except the bartender were ruffians.

When hearing the woman's story, the saloon man told the officers that her peculiar actions while in the bar seated between the two men was what caused the trouble. She seemed to be trying to communicate with him through facial expressions and hand movements, which he noticed but could not understand.

When asking the woman if there was something she was trying to tell him, the big man whipped out a

95

revolver and told him to mind his bartending and leave her alone. Then suspecting she was held against her will, he moved his white apron aside a bit to expose a gun he had trained on the big man.

Challenging the big escapee so coolly bluffed him and he pushed his revolver under his belt before the two left their stools in a hurry and pushed the woman ahead of them to go out through the batwing doors, with the saloon man vaulting the bar to assist them with their exit.

They knew he was on their tail and the big one, when outside, turned and fired a shot over the bartender's head, hoping to discourage and send him back, giving them time to get away in the boat.

Bruce, attempting to support the bartender's story, told of first seeing them at Buckhead Ridge before they stole his boat, and that he suspected the woman was with them against her will.

Upon hearing Bruce's voice, the Sheriff came forward while placing the beam of his flashlight on him, then lowering it he reached for Bruce's hand while anxiously saying to him, "Well! I'll be a punkin bug if it isn't Burl! What have you gotten yourself into now?"

Then he added, as if to the other officers, "Leave it to this catamount! When trouble erupts, anywhere, you can scratch around in the rubble and usually find old Burl Collins someplace!"

The woman then tried to explain to Bruce that she had no intentions of using the shotgun on the barkeep. But this was her first chance of escaping her captors, and she would have used the gun on anyone who tried to interfere.

In seeing Bruce in the light beam at close range, the escapees thought they recognized him as a man they knew in Raiford who was known to have escaped. But it

had now been three years, and after hearing the Sheriff call him Burl Collins, luckily for Bruce, they considered it a case of mistaken identity.

The Sheriff then told all who cared to hear, how Collins had handled the case of the egret plume poachers, and brought the ring leader, a trusted officer of the Audubon Society to jail. In a lower tone then, he mentioned there was another job he'd like to have old Burl work on for him but he did not elaborate.

CHAPTER 7

Other than the clack-clacking sound of the oarlocks in worn sockets, and the splashing of water occasionally when large mullet fish jumped above the surface near the boat to land back in the water on their side, no sound came out of the thick, early morning fog until the heavy chop-swish, chop-swish, chop-swishing sound of the large and powerful paddle-wheel of the steamboat was heard, when its position was only a short distance behind and rapidly bearing down on the little rowboat.

Leaving Fort Myers before any visible activity from the residents of the five-acre town, Bruce saw the steamboat still tied up at the town dock and suspected it would pass him before reaching La Belle. Hearing it coming now, there was no reason for alarm. But when the big boat drew closer and came into view, with it seemingly aimed directly toward him without mercy, he now realized he had been following the channel and his rowboat was in the path of this oversize bully.

With quick thinking to break with one oar and pull hard on the other, he barely managed to clear the way, where only he was aware of the closeness of the two ves-

sels when the long ship slipped past at arm's length —
only to, when the stern passed, have the big wheel nearly
pull his boat beneath the viciously chopping paddles.

With the freed kidnap victim and her two guns, the
shotgun and heavy revolver, aboard, Captain Johnson of
the big ship was maintaining a regular but tight schedule.
He had brought his steamboat *Lilly* out of port long
before daybreak, to brush unknowingly past the little
rowboat just before entering the narrow and crooked
Calooshatchee River on his return up the swift stream to
cross the big lake and reach Tantie where the ship's dis-
tinguished passenger would disembark before it continued to its northern terminus at the town of Kissimmee.

After passing the little boat to reach the mouth and
strong current of the river head-on, deep breathing
sounds of the mighty steam engine came strongly to
Bruce, where he also was laboring to match force with
the swifter water.

Bruce yesterday heard the Captain say that his ship
would leave Fort Myers promptly at daybreak. That was
fine for boats bound by a fixed schedule. But schedules
were not part of Bruce's daily fare, and he tried to avoid
becoming "bound" by anything in particular. He had left
earlier, hoping to be able to buck the strong current of the
river and reach Moore Haven before night.

Having no forethought of the dangers involved with
rowing his tiny boat in the channel with no running lights
during a fog of this sort, he was now well aware of what
could happen. Although the *Lilly* was ablaze with proper
lights, he only saw them when the brute was about ten
feet from him. But in any event he had now won another
round with one of these wheezing, floating castles that so
arrogantly and flauntingly imposed their size authority
over smaller craft, and was happy with the big bully

going along its way.

Current of the swift river, where it spilled into the wider body to join an outgoing Gulf tide, was felt by the "power" of the rowboat before reaching the mouth of the river.

Since the rowboat was used only for working the catfish trotlines there was no need for the sail. It was rolled around the mast and kept stashed across the seats along one side of the boat. When he was running in the woods to follow the lake's western shoreline, searching the surface of the water at every opportunity, he knew the sail would be visible for many miles, and when he was not able to locate it, he was fearful of the thieves thinking it was excess baggage and throwing it over the side.

When he found the boat on shore at the foot of the town dock with the sail and mast still onboard, he wondered if the two men knew what the bundle that made rowing a bit awkward was really for. But this thought was unfounded. The men were not all that ignorant. They knew a tall mast could be seen much farther than the low profile of a rowboat. And, too, with specific plans for the sail when the range became greater, they were not about to throw it over.

Bruce was bothered with no more marine traffic after the big steamboat nearly "done him in," and reaching the mouth of the river when the sun was dimly showing red through diminishing fog just above the treetops he was strongly considering using the sail. He mused, "Maybe now, with the sun up it will burn the fog out and the wind will rise, to not only make visibility better but with enough to round out the sail and assist my rowing against the strong current."

He had been concerned about his progress, knowing that while in the wider water, even if he could see land through the fog, the distance would be so great that he would not be able to gauge his speed. Now after entering the narrow and crooked river, with sometimes the bank almost within arm's reach, he would not have that problem.

But that problem was not as important as the one he had now acquired. To make any progress at all, while watching trees along the bank pass with the speed of a lazy snail, he was having to apply all the pressure the oars would stand. The current was so great that if he missed one stroke with an oar, the boat would not only stop, it would fall back several feet.

With the clearing of the fog came a mild wind. It was from the southwest, exactly from the direction he wanted. Now if it would become strong enough to be effective he would install the mast and sail. But how he would manage this? By the time this was accomplished, after the rowing stopped, the boat would be back out the mouth of the river.

Then Bruce saw a small patch of water where there was no current along the bank. It was behind the trunk of a large tree which, after centuries of standing to overlook the peaceful river, had given up life and fallen into the water to leave an eddy on the downstream side.

The area of still water behind the log was large enough to accommodate the small boat and he maneuvered it into the pocket, where he sat to rest and have a few bites of the "take-out" food the Sheriff had provided. Then after a bit more of enjoying the brief respite, he again took position at the oars and let the current pull his boat back into midstream.

As the sun rose higher the wind became stronger, and with slack now out of the sail he could feel the need for pressure on the oars to be a bit less. Trees were passing the boat faster. This created a state of mental relief. It was not long before the boat had gone around several of the sharp river bends, leaving it in a watery canyon between tall trees, and with no chance of the wind reaching his sail. He accepted this as just another of the unfortunate incidents which seemed to forever be his lot.

Leaving the sail up to catch the few and feeble puffs of wind which he found made contact for brief periods at some of the bends, giving some relief from his hard and steady laboring with the oars, he carried on, with the sun now across the top and settling earthward on the other side.

With the sun now touching the western horizon and the helpful wind zephyrs having retired for the night, the next bend Bruce managed to take his boat around exposed him to view the river crossing ferry at La Belle.

When reaching the ferry crossing and sidling into the guide cable and grasping to hold his boat from drifting until he could make it fast to a mooring post on the bank, there were no overnight accommodations in view. But that was the least of Bruce's worries. A dry river bank was all he needed. When Bruce saw the ferry tender standing near his small rain shack, and informing him of his intentions to camp there for the night, he was invited to stay in the rain shack. The tender was at that moment going off duty and would not return until daybreak.

The shack provided a safe and comfortable haven for the night but there was no campfire. He had nothing to cook. He left La Belle long before the ferry tender came back for duty. Bruce knew he was only about halfway between Fort Myers and where he would be free of the river's strong current when reaching the open water of the big lake at Moore Haven. He would camp overnight there if ever he reached it.

Battling a current which seemed forever determined to match its power with that of the friendly little rowboat, indeed, would be another day of hard rowing. But with most hardships there are bright spots. It seemed beyond every bend there was something different. A family of jet black coots may become frightened and rise off the surface, to run on the water for a short distance before becoming airborne. Tall blue herons were seen to take off gracefully on long wings from where they stood in shallow water. Turtles and gators, sliding into the water off logs and the river bank, and raccoons continuing their search for crawdads and unsuspecting minnows with no concern of the boat's presence.

In the late afternoon, with no food and nothing to stop for at lunch time, the little boat entered the open water of Lake Hicpochee, where a lively breeze reached to round out the sail, causing a smart list of the boat and Bruce to quickly move to the high side.

Using one oar for a rudder again, he relaxed to enjoy the short period of rest which he knew would end when passing through the lake to reach the narrows. But even so, the next spell of rowing would not be so long before he would reach the big cypress at Moore Haven.

Buying no food in La Belle, he had eaten nothing after last night at the ferry when he finished off the last of the food he brought from Fort Myers. When tying up at the big tree a short time before sunset, he hurried on to Parkinson's store lest it would be closed for the day and he would have to go through the night without food.

Tonight there would not be the luxury of a roof over him as in La Belle. Only the long moss-draped boughs of the ancient cypress would shield him from the stars.

Even with his boat only a few feet from him tonight, losing it to thieves still registered strongly with him,

causing him to resort to a system he had used before —
sleeping with the mooring line lying on the ground under
him.

The clack-clacking sound of oarlocks could be heard
again when light rays first began showing in an eastern
sky faintly, through the stillness of a gray mist of early
morning fog, as the little craft made its way from Lake
Hicpochee toward Lake Okeechobee. When burning
through the fog to cast light on the river bank under the
silent but friendly old tree, the sun showed only a perpet-
ual welcome extended to weary travelers who may care to
tarry.

Full of enthusiasm, and with the day just beginning,
Bruce now had his boat back and was in familiar waters,
where the increasing southwest wind filled the boat's sail
to the limit and was driving the little craft at a lively
pace. This caused a steep list to starboard and Bruce was
having to ride the highest point of the boat. What was
most important, however, was that he was heading home.

With the sun rising ever higher, while the wind continued to strengthen, the little boat was listing more
strongly and chopping a bit from waves which had built
higher with the stronger wind. But even with the stronger
wind and the boat having no keel or centerboard to hold
it stable, it was accepting the command of its master
gracefully and sailing like a veteran while covering mile
after mile.

Everything was now in Bruce's favor. The wind was
holding steady. His little boat was cruising faster, and
with the way it was climbing the waves, it appeared to be
enjoying the journey as well as he. And don't forget the
most important part — there was no rowing to be done.

Because of all this, Bruce decided, instead of hug-
ging the shoreline around the western side for the longer

but safer way home as normally would have been done with a boat this small, he would follow the short course, straight from Moore Haven to Buckhead Ridge.

With his ship sailing gallantly, he tied off the sail at the proper angle to collect wind that would drive it faster, and moved to a better position of relaxation, where he just sat and dreamed...dreamed of foreign seas touching on enchanted lands, lands waiting to be discovered and explored.

Bruce had no compass, but the weather was clear and after going beyond the sight of land, he was able to use the sun to stay on his desired course, which he calculated would put him in close vicinity of his home on Buckhead with much daylight to spare. Even if he missed his target, he knew the tall cypress trees on the ridge would be visible from several miles offshore, allowing for early adjustment.

When he and Fannie eloped from her home on the eastern shore to return to his tribe on Buckhead across the upper end of the lake, it was Bruce's first venture beyond the sight of land. But that distance was not as great as the voyage he was now attempting. And, even though alone this time, there was no feeling of loneliness — only of accomplishment as he sat relaxed watching his little ship gracefully handling the small waves while the wind held steady pressure against a well rounded sail.

Favoring the high side so that his weight would compensate for a mast which was now standing at a wide angle, idleness encouraged his thinking. He was thinking of what the Sheriff had said about needing his help with a problem, and possibly, in the near future, going back to Fort Myers to assist him. The Sheriff had not said what he needed help with. If he had explained the nature of the mission, Bruce's urge to participate may have been disappeared.

Cruising steadily onward, while also appearing happy with the voyage, the little boat was holding course and performing equal to any tall ship of any period on any sea. With Bruce far, far away in his own dreams, no thought was given to time. It was not long before he might as well have been on one of the foreign seas in his dreams. Without noticing, the boat was now so far out into open water that, with the now higher waves and low profile of his craft, there was no land in sight in any direction. When he first realized this, the thought was no less than frightening. With his past ventures on this vast body of water, he had never been alone this far from land. But even so, there always has to be a first for everything. And there was no more danger out here than one hundred yards from shore as long as he had a good ship under him. Anyway, he was into it now and would just have to hold tight and see the thing through.

After cruising on and on with nothing but water in sight, he had no idea of his position until a short time before sunset when coming back from his never-never land to look west when he saw the tall cypress trees that he knew so well. His negligence in keeping track of his position had caused him to miss target by several miles.

Realizing now that while sleeping at the helm he had about passed his home without altering the course, he quickly pushed the tiller end of the oar he was using for a rudder to starboard, causing the bow of his boat to suddenly point to port toward the west and tall trees.

Making a radical change in course without adjusting the sail to compensate for a wind which would now have to touch the sail set at a different angle to drive the craft in a cross wind was a grave mistake. When the boat turned for the wind to catch a broad sail with full force, with the boat having no keel or centerboard to hold her, she rolled on edge with sail and mast lying flat on the water.

Having been overboard in the lake many times, this seemed nothing to become disturbed over. But when recovering from the sudden dunking to stand and take control of the situation he found there was nothing to stand on. He knew then that the trees on the ridge were much farther than they first appeared, and he was overboard in water much deeper than ever before.

And at the moment the situation seemed to be reversed. The lake was in control of him. To say he was disturbed, when describing Bruce's present condition, was putting it mildly. He was downright frightened. How was he to turn the boat upright and bail the water from it with nothing to stand on? But there was no time to waste in pondering his predicament.

In seemingly bottomless water, and with nothing else that would support his weight beyond the reach of critters which he knew inhabited this lake, there was nothing left but to move with haste.

Quickly swimming to the bow of the up-edged boat, he grabbed the mast with both hands and placed his feet against the boat, where he pulled the pole from its socket. This freed the boat to roll back to an upright position, but it was now filled with water.

When the sudden and unexpected roll of the boat dumped him into the lake he managed to hang onto the oar he was using for a rudder. It had floated nearby while he removed the mast and sail. After placing it in the water-filled boat, he moved quickly to retrieve the other oar and bailing box from where they had drifted, several yards away.

Even with the boat now full of water it did not sink. It was made of wood and floated just under the water's surface.

When returning to the boat with the oar and bailing box, he saw it was rocking from waves washing across it. Swimming then to the side from which the waves were coming, and while still swimming, he raised that side to where the waves would not pass over it.

When he did this, a sizable volume of water poured out the other side. When having to let go after holding the weight as long as he was able, there was an inch of free board above water at the lowest point, with other parts even higher above water. This encouraged him until the next wave filled the boat again.

At a time like this, encouragement or not, what he did showed possibilities. Losing no time, he applied a mighty effort to raise the boat even higher, and held it longer allowing more water to pour from it. The next wave tried but was not quite able to go over the side.

He then started dipping water over the side with double-time speed. Racing with the larger waves which sometimes dumped more water into the boat, it took some fast dipping before it became noticeable that he was slowly gaining.

With now seeing that his efforts were not in vain, he expected to win the battle, but did not dare let up with his dipping lest an extremely large wave came to cancel everything that was accomplished. There was a little more freeboard above water now and none of the waves were coming over. With this progress came further encouragement.

With his interest consumed with getting all his boat back on top of the water, it was only when the tail of an alligator slammed against his back that he returned to the

awareness of the danger of being in water with the critters. It was also then that he thought of his Owl Head
revolver in his side pocket two feet under water.

The gator was not a large one. It was only about four
feet in length but it was aggressive, with a desire to
attack its prey a second time, as it came toward Bruce
with its head above water.

This was a fearful sight and a problem with seemingly no options for solving. If he attempted to crawl over
the side into the boat, it surely would result in sinking it
again. There was the gun. It was that or nothing.

With no faith whatsoever in water-soaked ammunition, he quickly drew the gun from his pocket and

brought it to the surface where he poured water from the barrel and cylinders, then saw it drain slowly from the breechlock by the time the gator's head was only a few inches beyond arm's length. In a state of extreme desperation he pointed the gun and squeezed the trigger. The gun fired, killing the gator instantly.

Seeing the reptile roll onto its back and display its white belly, and with blood starting to discolor the water around its head, Bruce was reminded that it was with gators as with sharks — fresh blood from one attracted others and made them more vicious and aggressive.

He knew that with the red water spreading ever wider around him and the dead gator, his period of safety in the water was very short. Maybe if in some way he could get inside the boat, the water within would support most of his weight while he dipped to raise the boat sides high enough, where no gators would be tempted to crawl over the side to reach him.

But this was out. His fast dipping had only resulted in raising the boat's side to where it appeared possible to float it again. If he attempted to climb over now, even at the stern, all his work would be wasted. He had no choice but to dip, dip, dip.

While working as fast as humanly possible under the adverse conditions, he watched with increasing enthusiasm as the sides of the boat raised with seemingly the speed of a growing tree.

After considerably more time was spent in his stressful labor, a little more free board was showing but not nearly enough to take a chance of sinking the boat again by trying to get inside. He would just have to keep dipping and hoping.

His hopes were short-lived. Only a few more gallons of water were back into the lake, with no more free board showing, before gator heads could be seen on the surface in several places, from ten to thirty yards from the swamped boat.

Bruce noticed the gators which were on the side of him where the dead gator lay floating, were the ones the farthest away. With this fact established, an idea was born. While the sunken boat protected his other side, he quickly swam to where the dead gator had drifted and brought it closer to him.

While the boat protected him on the one side, the white belly of the dead gator floating high in the water near him kept the others away until about half the water was out of the boat, where it now appeared he might be able to get inside without sinking the boat.

Swimming to the stern and bringing his protective gator with him, he gently climbed to sit on the stern seat with his feet hanging in the water behind the boat.

With the oars having already been placed within the sides of the sunken boat and now floating above the seats, when Bruce was satisfied after dipping a little more water, he took up the oars and maneuvered the boat to retrieve the mast and sail from where they had drifted from the power of the wind and waves.

Even though the boat now would support his weight, the water in it made it anything but stable. When he leaned over the side to reach and lift the floating mast, his weight along with water rushing to that side would have rolled the boat over again if he had not quickly favored it by going in head-first to relieve it of that much weight.

Scrambling to reach the stern where he could gain safety of the boat again, he was in position to climb up when a gator which had been following beneath the boat latched onto his right hand.

Feeling pain when the powerful jaws applied bone-crushing pressure, Bruce felt a fainting sensation and knew his hand was seriously wounded, but try as hard as he did, there was no pulling away from the reptile. He knew, too, the nature of the things were, after getting a grip on their catch they would roll and drown it. This would be attempted at any moment.

His revolver had fired before but it had been under water all this much longer. Anyway, he was helpless. He was right-handed. His gun was in his pocket on the right side, and the gator had hold of his right hand.

Then he felt the gator move, surely preparing to make its killing roll. This left Bruce with no option but to try something he had never done before. His mind was racing for something, anything, but there was no time left, not even for thought.

But in times when it's life or death, things are done without thought. Moves are made unconsciously. With his left hand, Bruce managed to reach across his body and draw the gun from his right side pocket.

Having never fired the gun left-handed, along with his bearing increased pain to lift his right arm so that the gator's head would be above the surface, one shot was all he would have time for, and only seconds before certain death.

Upon impact of the bullet the gator released Bruce's hand and turned onto its back in death, leaving Bruce free to climb over the stern into the boat, and to safety from the others which the sound of the gunshot had caused to momentarily submerge.

Feeling no pain in his hand after it was free, he was rejoicing until he realized instead of pain there was no feeling at all. Knowing then what this meant, he became frightened. He was afraid to raise his hand to the surface where he could see it, but in order to climb over into the boat, this would have to be.

Reaching the stern now, he grasped the top side with his left hand and without looking, raised his right hand and placed it along side the left. But it fell away. There was no grip to hold the right hand in place. Only the thumb, ring, and little fingers made any attempt to hang onto the boat.

Now realizing that to ignore the wound was not going to help the situation, he laid the injured hand back on the boat again and saw that the first and middle fingers were about bitten off.

No blood was coming from the wound, and for this he was thankful. But with no grip in the hand, how was he to get into the boat?

With the gators having gained confidence and surfaced again, and all pointed toward him, with the feeble help of the uninjured fingers on his right hand, in addition to help with his left hand, he managed to pull himself up and over the stern panel, where he sat for a moment overcoming the exhaustion of his extreme effort.

Now frantically handling the bailing box left-handed, while becoming nauseated, he managed to dip the remainder of the water from the boat. Then with his left hand pulling an oar like a paddle, while his wounded right hand supported the upper end, he brought the boat back to the mast and sail where, with his left hand, he managed to roll them into the boat and rest them across the seats along one side.

Noticing then that the strain of getting the heavy water soaked sail and mast into the boat had caused the wound to start bleeding profusely, he became more nauseated.

Becoming very disturbed over this, he knew, without

delay, something would have to be done to prevent his bleeding to death, but he had nothing (or seemingly no way) to help himself with. The line on the boat's bow could be used to make a tourniquet, but with only one hand he would not be able to arrange it.

Finally, and now in a state of nearly total desperation, he removed his wet shirt and, with teeth and one hand, wound it tightly around the bleeding hand.

"This may not stop the bleeding entirely," he thought, "but maybe it will stem the flow enough that I will not become too weak to manage the boat in some sort of a fashion and reach home."

Bruce estimated the trees he saw on Buckhead were five miles away at the most. But five miles, with a brisk wind coming at you from broadside to blow your boat off course, could be a long distance, even for an uninjured navigator.

Taking up one oar and attempting to at least prevent his boat being blown farther away than its present position, he very clumsily managed to keep the bow pointed in the desired direction for a spell, but with now not able to even partly grasp the upper end of the oar with two fingers as before the shirt bandage, his efforts were more awkward and he quickly became tired and had to stop to rest, only to see his boat turn and follow the course of the wind.

This whole unfortunate tragedy had consumed more time than Bruce realized. The trees on Buckhead was now silhouetted against a red and rapidly setting summer sun.

He tried again and harder to control the boat with a one-handed paddle, and gained a little on the distance separating him from home, but he also was now racing with the sun.

115

But putting strain on the wounded hand while trying to support the top of the paddle oar caused bleeding to start again. The makeshift shirt bandage was now saturated and red. Loss of blood and the unsightly bandage were causing greater nausea.

Darkness began hovering over the lake, and realizing that his weakness might prevent his carrying on with trying to reach home, he needed to conserve his remaining strength to endure a long and lonely night on the water, with his only hopes for the wind to change during the night, and the beginning of another day would finding it blowing his boat toward home.

But Bruce was not ready to surrender. Gently placing his oar across the seats, he stood erect facing toward where he knew the trees stood in silent darkness, towering over his cheekee where Fannie would be waiting and watching for his return.

The distance to the trees had only been shortened enough to see there was some gain, but still they were a long way off. While standing he thought, "If only the wind would cease, maybe even at this great distance I could make my voice heard." But he knew the wind doesn't always stop at sunset, and his continuing weakness would not allow time for long delays.

Trying to stand taller while still facing westward, he placed his open left hand beside his face to shield his voice from the crosswind. With all his remaining strength, he alternately and repeatedly sounded the nature calls of his two Indian fishing partners, Toby and Louis. Then Bruce switched and called and called using the nature sound the Braves bestowed upon him when he first became one of their "Brothers" — the call he, and only he, could claim and use, that of the Bob White Quail.

His voice seemed to be carrying only a short distance, and Bruce became weaker until his legs would not support his weight. He sat again on the stern seat. Then feeling very tired and wanting to rest, he let himself slip from the seat to lie in the wet bottom of the boat.

Darkness had now long set in, and while the faithful little boat bobbed gently on ever diminishing waves of the mighty body of water, only the night sounds of low flying loons or osprey could be heard.

Bruce was semiconscious. He was in a stupor. He was now dreaming fitfully, and heard a voice. The voice sounded close: "Brucie." Then he heard it again, louder: "Brucie." And again. And in feeling a hand on his face he opened his eyes to see Toby in the boat with him, while Louis sat in a dugout close along the side holding the crafts together.

With still mind enough to realize his physical condition had now deteriorated to a state of delirium, he accepted the presence of the Indians as no less than hallucinations, and lapsed back into nothingness.

CHAPTER 8

When he opened his eyes to the sharp, slanting rays of a summer sun, reaching him where he lay under the thatched roof of his cheekee, Bruce saw Fannie watching him from where she sat on the edge of his slatted bed rack, and knew this was just another illusion. After a moment of watching her, he saw movement and suspected she may be real. When she saw he was awake, Fannie touched his face gently. In a low voice he called her name. Reaching then for her hand, he grasped it firmly and held on, before closing his eyes and nothing more was said.

Awakening again after a short period, Bruce saw his hand done up in a clean and professional bandage, and turned his face to Fannie with words trying to form.

Quickly placing her hand over his mouth to prevent questions she knew he was trying to ask, Fannie said to him, "No! Not now! After you have had food we will talk."

It was near noon when Bruce awakened this time, to find Fannie was not with him. Only his dog, Tag, was in sight where it sat on the ground with its nose and front paws resting on the edge of his bed, watching his master closely.

Hearing sound behind him, Bruce turned over to see Fannie working over a low campfire, preparing food — his first since before leaving Moore Haven yesterday before there was light.

Using his left hand, and with no conversation between them Bruce ate heartily of the warm food while studying the bandage and sling on his right hand and arm. He was waiting, a bit impatiently, for answers to questions he knew she was aware he wanted to ask.

"Yes, Dear!" Fannie broke the silence with, when seeing his anxiety building. "He had to! Both of them! You were out there so long after it happened, gangrene was starting and the medicine man thought it not wise to take chances of attempting to control it and maybe, after possibly losing the battle, having to remove the entire hand to stop its spreading further! This way, you have lost only the first and middle fingers. He took them off at the upper joint."

"You said I was out there so long after it happened! What happened? I haven't been able to tell anyone what happened!"

"We don't know what happened! That's what I'm anxious to hear! But no one had to tell the medicine man what wounded you! He said nothing except a gator could inflict such a wound!"

After a moment of silence, while maintaining a puzzled expression, Bruce asked, "But how did the medicine man know I needed help? How did I get home? Did the wind change and blow my boat ashore?"

"No! We all were sitting around the campfire awaiting your return, until it became late and everyone but Toby and I retired to their cheekees. Toby then suggested I retire and he would keep the fire going, that you would be able to locate the camp from offshore if you were trying to reach home at night! But I did not retire, and only a short time later he quickly became alert and sprang to his feet, where he trained an ear toward the lake, and after a brief moment eagerly said, 'I heard it again! I heard it! I faintly heard it! I heard Bob White! No quail heard at night! No quail on water!'

"He turned to me then and said anxiously, 'Brucie in trouble! I go! I go! You stay, keep fire going! I wake Louis. We go quick!'

"Immediately after they left in a dugout boat I alerted the medicine man and he built up the fire before we went to wait on shore. We waited and waited, and after what seemed an eternity, we heard the sound of oarlocks. Shortly thereafter the two boats came to the dock where, in darkness, we hurriedly lifted and carried you to the medicine man's cheekee!"

"But I don't remember any surgery!"

"I'm sure of that!! You were first given a sedative potion, and with not knowing what was going on, due to your already weakened condition, you readily swallowed it, after which you cooperated very nicely!"

"Cooperated! What did I do?"

"It was what you did not do that helped! The sedative put you completely out of business and you knew nothing until today when the hot morning sun awakened you!"

Approaching quietly from behind, the medicine man interrupted them as he placed a hand on Bruce's shoulder, reaching with the other to lift the bandaged hand and inspect it and the arm for swelling or fever, before he asked, "Umph!..Sore?"

"No!" Bruce answered. "No feeling at all!""Umph!

Hand healing! I come back sundown!"

And he did come back, sundown and sunrise, too, for several more days without yielding to pleas from Bruce to be allowed to go back to fishing, not even to accompany his partners when they collect their catch, even if he would not touch a fish or line.

But during his "house arrest," where he was supposed to be confined to his cheekee or the near vicinity, and while fretting more as the days passed, he became very much concerned with the daily instructions of his doctor. Seeing activity at the fishing dock and since the doctor was not in sight, Bruce exercised his Indian know-how and managed to reach the dock undetected.

The doctor became more aware of his patient stretching the privileges granted, to the point where now when he wanted to check the wound for progress or to change a bandage, he first looked for Bruce at the dock.

This routine schedule continued until the bandage was removed, exposing the hand. But, no...less than a hand, creating a state of deep depression for Bruce.

When finally released from the medicine man's restrictions, Bruce lost no time in getting back to the catfish lines. He only had to try once to discover he was no longer able to handle the boat. The remaining two fingers and thumb could not grip the oar strong enough to produce the necessary power on that side. To his Indian fishing partners, this seemed no problem. They would be happy to switch the regular work arrangement. Bruce could now help Toby man the trotlines and Louis would handle the boat.

The new arrangement worked only long enough to receive a fair trial before it also was found to be too much. Bruce could not grip and hold the heavy trotline on his side of the boat while his left hand (uninjured) raised the drop lines and removed the catch. Watching Bruce become more frustrated with his failing efforts to do his part, the Indians wanted to help, but what was there to do? Each had a distinctive and separate part in their operation, and there was no way for one man to handle both trotlines when they were on opposite sides of the boat. Neither could one man work a line and at the same time maneuver the boat.

While silently attempting to help, the Braves, as well as Bruce, realized that the futility of their efforts was simply bringing on frustration for them as well. It became apparent that if the fishing was to continue, something different would have to be done. Bruce made the necessary move.

Discussing it with Fannie after work that day, it was decided maybe for the time being, until his hand healed and was strong again, they should go back to Fort Myers where he could help the Sheriff with the problem he spoke of, if it was something that could be done with only one hand. But on second thought, this was out because he would not be able to row the boat that distance.

Remembering then, a few weeks ago in Tantie they saw a motorboat for sale. If the boat was still available, this may solve their problem. Becoming so enthused over this possibility, Bruce did not wait until the following day when he would again be trying to carry his part of the load. He went to the cheekees of the two Braves that very night and informed them of his intentions.

Fannie was anything except an expert at rowing a boat. But the following morning, after leaving Buckhead at daybreak, she managed in a zigzag manner to buck the strong current of Taylor Creek and nose the little boat up to the dock shortly after noon.

The reason for not buying the boat in the first place

was the shortage of cash, and they were no better off now, except this time, the urgent need of the boat prepared them to try for a lower price, or pay what they had and the balance later.

When they reached the dock they saw the boat tied up at the same location as before, but now without the sale sign attached. This took the wind out of their sail, causing momentarily disillusionment. But since the nature of neither was to be faint at heart, they soon located the owner of the boat and learned that there was no one interested and he removed the sign. He suggested if they were interested in buying it, make an offer.

The boat was old but sound, and to Bruce it seemed very much alive. It would go places under its own power, and with him having not ridden in a motorboat recently, it gave him a strange and sensational feeling.

The thing was purely a thoroughbred lake boat, with its long swayback sweep melding into an unreasonable and stupid-appearing boat. It was equipped with a heavy, single-cylinder inboard engine that needed to be halted and then cranked backward for reverse.

The critical looking thing had a pipe coming out its side, where the popping sound from the engine and its cooling water came out in rapid but short spurts, creating the sound of shooting large firecrackers in a bathtub.

After the slow and delicate business of bickering until the price matched their savings, and to the former owner's satisfaction that Bruce understood the unnatural peculiarities of the thing, and would be able to make it yield to his command, they were left to themselves, where they visited the store to buy much needed supplies to take back.

While standing at a counter where a clerk was helping with the selection of a purchase, they heard a voice from behind where another clerk was asked if he knew a Burl Collins who may be living in the area. Upon hearing the name "Burl" Bruce thought the man was from down Fort Myers way, and he turned to make his presence known, but drew back quickly when recognizing the man as an inmate he saw while in prison. Bruce was saved by the poor lighting in the building.

With his back turned toward the man again, Bruce continued with the examination of the article he planned to buy. He then heard the man, after further talk with the clerk and before leaving the store, ask the way to Buckhead Ridge.

Turning away from the counter to watch the man leave, Bruce followed him to the front and saw him go into the fish house where he knew the purpose of the visit was to inquire about him.

The ex-con knew Bruce's correct name, and had he inquired of him in that manner, those in the store and the fish house would have quickly pointed him out. But with the ex-con thinking "Burl" was the handle Bruce had used after escaping, no one would know him otherwise.

Bruce knew if the man had seen his face he would have recognized him as the inmate who was successful where so many others failed. But now, with inquiring of him as "Burl" instead of Bruce, he was totally stumped. He couldn't quite make that one out.

For the brief period Bruce stayed in prison he did not cultivate friendships with any of the other inmates and hardly recognized them by name, except at roll call.

Then Bruce remembered the two escapees from Raiford who stole his boat and were captured in Fort Myers, who were most certainly sent back to prison. There could be only one answer: the two escapees had arrived back in Raiford before this man finished his sentence and was released. And the purpose of his visiting this area was double-revenge for the other two and the hundred dollar reward for himself.

Finishing their shopping they left the store under stress of maybe bumping into the man and having to deal with him in some manner, but the man was nowhere in sight and they managed to reach their boat and get out of town.

Now, with supplies for their voyage and the exuberance of a child with a new toy over the ownership of the slow, steady and very unstately lake fisherman's boat with a style like none others on earth, they cruised majestically back out the twisting creek on their way home, with the tiny rowboat following willfully at the end of a stout rope.

Since living in lake country for these past four years and viewing the "high-head" lake boats from afar and up close, Bruce had wondered about their awful shape, but had come to the conclusion that they were built this way simply to maintain a "fisherman" style for identification if sighted at a distance by other fishermen.

But now, after his bout with the playful wind and pesky gators, he realized that during a real blow, the waves on this lake can reach heights that would make even this boat seem to be a peanut shell.

Upon arriving home with their new boat, they were told by the Braves that a stranger in a motorboat had been there asking about a "Burl Collins." But not knowing anyone by that name, they were not able to help him, and where he went after leaving them, they did not know.

Bruce now understood where the man had acquired the information about him being in lake country, and that he was seen working catfish rigs with the Indians at Buckhead. He knew the man would now go on to Fort

Myers in search of him after not finding him here. Bruce also suspected the man was told by his informers to contact the Sheriff in Fort Myers and tip him off about Bruce Coggins escaping from Raiford and living down this way under the assumed name of Burl Collins. Maybe the Sheriff would appreciate the information and help him earn and collect the reward.

And, too, believing the man would come back to the north end of the lake again in search of him, this time using his correct name, he and Fannie decided to pack their boat, including Tag and their pet coon "Varmint" and leave earlier than planned. They would leave tomorrow at daybreak to cross the big lake, this time around the shoreline, and follow the swift and crooked river back to the west coast.

If fortunate enough to reach Tice, where the saltwater from the Gulf begins, and just short of Fort Myers, they planned to hole up for a spell and maybe assist their mullet fishermen friends with their nets, while hoping to miss this man as they did another bounty hunter. Or at least they would maintain their base there until checking out the situation in Fort Myers. Had the ex-con already been there and talked with the Sheriff?

They knew the man was using a motorboat, but knew nothing of the type or color. To play it safe when passing other boats, Bruce would lie flat on the floor of their boat, out of sight. The man from Raiford had never seen Fannie and would not suspect that this Indian woman alone in her boat with a dog and pet coon, had any connection with Bruce Coggins. But with Bruce on the floor and Fannie not able to identify the man, they had no way of knowing if one of the several craft they had met with only one man aboard was the one they were trying to elude.

After no contact with the man while cruising leisurely along the western shoreline in their new-found love, a boat which seemed very large and traveled constantly, with much more speed than they were used to, they decided when reaching Moore Haven it probably would be safe to tie up at the big cypress near the mouth of the narrow river and make camp for the night.

When the boat was moored up against the bank, where their tent would be erected under the tree, Bruce tied a small line, which would not be noticed, to the boat and ran it along the ground to the tent, where it was placed under his bed and back across the top. If any attempt was made to move the boat away during the night, he certainly would know of it.

The small tent was large enough for two people and one dog. It also would have accommodated one coon if he had so desired but Varmint had other ideas. His meddlesome nature kept him outside exploring the river and lake shore until a short time before they planned to leave, when he crawled under to settle down for his daytime sleeping.

During the night they heard several boats passing in both directions, but there was no way of knowing if any one of them was their man heading to Buckhead in search of Bruce. But even if he did pass during the night, they knew he would not have connected the boat tied against the bank with Bruce, because when he was at Buckhead before, they were in Tantie to buy the boat.

Their tent was fine when on dry land, but that was not the case tonight. There was rain in Moore Haven all day yesterday, making the muck under the tree soft. During his diving to the floor when seeing other boats yesterday Bruce noticed their boat floor was wide and long, and had much more space than the tent provided.

The size of the boat floor sparked an idea, so when they were in Parkinson's store early the following morning to pick up more supplies, they included a tarpaulin large enough to cover all the boat behind the bulkhead at the engine box. Bruce then rigged a pole which could be installed when needed, that would support the tarpaulin in the middle like a roof top which would shed rain off each side.

Leaving Moore Haven when the sun was well up and establishing its strength, and cruising the crooked and

narrow, but beautiful Caloosahatchee, they were not long in reaching Lake Hicpochee to find a gentle wind blowing across the open lake reminding Bruce of when he passed this way before to enjoy the sail carrying his rowboat along at a brisk rate of speed. But this time there was no need for sail nor oars, which left freedom to enjoy the many sights of nature.

Passing through the lake to follow the river again, there were alligators and turtles sliding off the bank and logs into the water just ahead of the boat. Water fowl — jet black coots, colorful wood ducks and long-legged crane among many species — were less frightened with this boat. They observed many coons where they fished the shallow water at the river's edge with their front feet, but the busy coons paid no attention when the boat moved steadily past with no movement from its occupants.

After traveling such a great distance without encountering their tormentor, while being treated to the soul-soothing sights of so many wonderful wild creatures of nature, their thoughts of Bruce possibly having to return to prison had very much subsided.

With this longer boat there were closed compartments providing storage for more provisions. In Parkinson's store they bought enough canned and staple food to last several weeks if it became necessary to conserve and, in thinking about it, decided to purchase a large keg with faucet, for storing fresh water.

They knew, beginning at the end of the narrow part of the river, before reaching Fort Myers, they would be in saltwater and could not dip a drink of water from beside the boat as was practiced by fishermen in the big lake. Also while in the store, with Fannie busy selecting cooking utensils which would fit into compartments on the boat, Bruce was buying fishing tackle suitable for saltwater. He also filled the boat's fuel tank, so that they would have enough to reach La Belle.

The flow of the river was toward Fort Myers, and the boat engine was offering no complaints. With help of the current it was able to propel the boat much faster than when in still water, and by mid-day when nosing the boat into a niche in the bank where they would have lunch under large live oaks which spread their long and moss-draped branches half across the river, they had traveled quite a distance from the big cypress at the river's head.

Bruce's hand was healing normally, but he still was not able to use it for anything strenuous, not even to push it into his pocket. He knew that after more progress this would be possible, but he would not be able to draw and use his revolver for protection because he had no trigger finger.

Knowing this was going to be a permanent handicap, he switched the gun to his left side where, with not wanting the shock of firing explosions to maybe pass through his body to reach the wounded hand, he had been making dry hauls, hoping to develop a left-hand draw equal to that of his right.

Now, after more healing, the wound felt strong enough to stand a little shock, so while in Moore Haven he bought fresh ammunition for the purpose of getting in some live practice. There was no better place to begin than in this remote hammock of sable palm and live oaks.

After considerable time practicing this, while becoming fairly accurate and proficient of speed, he was tiring of this first practice with live ammunition. Varmint was called down from the top of a sable palm where Tag had playfully chased him, and where he was now busy with ripe cabbage berries, to board the boat so that they could depart.

With their lunch stop under the massive oaks lasting longer than intended, and with not getting started again until mid-afternoon, the sun had descended below the treetops when the ferry at La Belle came into view as they rounded a bend in the river.

La Belle, at that period in time, was nothing more than a watering hole and overnight holding pens for cattle on drives to Fort Myers for shipment, and where saddle horses were given a chance to wallow while their riders were in the busiest place in the hamlet partaking of the tried and true elixirs which make a cowpoke's drab lot in life endurable. Despite all this, or maybe in part because of it, this lazy, peaceful little trading post cast a spell of fascination, something unexplainable but with strong effect. And so it had been with Bruce ever since first passing this way. Something magnetic seemed to be in force.

Men were standing at the town side of the ferry landing and a motorboat was seen to leave and go downriver, just ahead of Bruce who was cutting his boat engine and heading the craft into the sloping bank at the feet of the conversing men.

After throwing a line to the group of men, expecting assistance with beaching the boat so that the current would not take it away, it was the local Sheriff who caught the line, the one Bruce recognized as the lawman who captured and took away from the net racks Bruce's first bounty hunter.

With the surprise of not expecting to see the man still in office after such a long time, Bruce's thought was to play it cool and pretend not to know him. But that kite would not fly. In his usual strong voice, hardly before the rope was in his hands, the Sheriff said, "Well, well! I'll be a hundered-down cowpoke, if it isn't my old mullet scrapping friend, Burl Collins!"

Remembering that in these parts everyone knew him by this handle, Bruce sprang from the boat to shore where he reached for the lawman's hand, and to hear him continue.

"And will mysteries ever cease? Here we are again, back where we left off. That boat you see rounding the bend down yonder is carrying another man searching for the same escaped convict that the other fellow tried to frame you with, Bruce Coggins!"

This type of thing Bruce had learned to live with long ago, and he was sure with his ability to master such situations in the past, his friendly expression did not change when suddenly surprised by the Sheriff's presence and remarks. Both he and Fannie now knew that somewhere between there and where they would meet their friends again at the net racks, they would have to ask the gentle river to reinvest them with the names, Burl and Frances Collins.

CHAPTER 9

After hearing this from the Sheriff and watching the boat until it rounded a bend and out of their view, adrenaline became very active with both Bruce and Fannie, and they were sure the effects were registering in their faces. This was too close for comfort, although they tried to pretend otherwise.

With an attempt to relieve the tension, shortly after leaving the Sheriff, they pulled into an eddy along the shore line where they tied up and made camp for the night.

Aided by the river current the boat reached the colony of mullet fishermen before noon the following day.

When the net racks came into view Bruce noticed they were entirely covered with drying nets and the boats were all in port, something that should not be at this time of day. Upon reaching the cottage of the fishing crew chief, Ed Weller, they learned that the market for mullet was gutted and there would be no more fishing until the oversupply was cleared up.

After enjoying several days of visiting with the fishing folks while they loafed, with no end to the market glut in sight and with their supply of money becoming short, Bruce and Fannie decided to check with the Sheriff to see if he still wanted Bruce to help with the problem he mentioned to "Burl."

The Sheriff was happy to see "Burl" again and glad to hear he was here to help and, too, was anxious for him to get right on with the assignment. But the Sheriff was not in favor of Fannie going with him on this dangerous mission. Although when it was explained that she had no place to stay except with him in the boat, and that she and Tag (and Varmint, of course) would have to accompany "Burl" or he could not accept the job, the Sheriff relented and deputized Fannie also so that she would be along as an officer with authority, if needed.

With the official action over, the Sheriff said to Bruce, "Burl, I'm going to let you and Francis go down there and bring them varmints out of their shell stealing game, but first I owe you an apology! Those two prison escapees who stole your boat and you captured for me, escaped from my jail, too, before they could be sent back to Raiford! But you go ahead, Burl, and bring those shell poachers in. I won't let that happen with any more crooks I lock up!"

Bruce was told where the tree snail area was and which prong of the waterways in the ten thousand islands to follow to reach the creek that would provide a safe and secret harbor to leave the boat while trekking overland through the jungles to find their headquarters.

The balance of that day was spent in making "blind" preparations for the journey into an area which was strange territory to Bruce. He had covered much of the Big Cypress area on foot but not in this section.

Bruce had been in the maze of waterways among the

islands before, but at that time he was lost, and finding his way out was by accident. But now, after this trip, if he could follow the directions of the Sheriff, he would be better acquainted with the channels and would not have to depend on his prisoners piloting the boat out, as he did before.After agreeing to help the Sheriff, Bruce and Fannie did not go back to stay with their fishermen friends that night. They stayed in Fort Myers to sleep under the newly rigged tarpaulin again, and were on their way to the islands when light was sufficient to travel without running lights.

There would be no problem with the first part of the trip. Bruce had passed this way before in daylight and he would remember the various landmarks along the shore line, even if sometimes at a great distance.As the cool, early morning temperature gave way to the sun's heat gaining in intensity, the boat party cruised along leisurely watching the fat mullet jump to drag a trail of water behind them, only to flop back into the mirror smooth surface, with the sailing pelicans that appeared to be shot from a trap and did not need wings searching the boat below for friendly fishermen. Bruce was at the tiller on the stern seat when suddenly, he stood to hold the tiller stick between his knees while the appearance of deep concern developed on his face.

Fannie saw Bruce's anxious concern and came to stand beside him silently, while her puzzled eyes were asking, "What is wrong?"

Bruce reminded her that the two escapees were not sent back to prison before the man who was searching for him as "Burl Collins" served his time and was released. To Bruce, the fact that this man knew about Burl Collins meant only one thing — he and the two escapees had been in contact after they broke out of the Fort Myers jail, and now the man was a self proclaimed bounty hunter trying to collect the reward for Bruce's capture, where Bruce would be sent back to prison to serve out his sentence, with more time added for escaping.

Being in salt water now, there were different wild creatures to be seen. There were the big-beaked pelicans gliding along smoothly in formation as they looked down at the boat to see if there were fish, making it worth their while to follow the boat for the culls that may be thrown out, and the smaller, silver gray ones that just sat on the water to bob up and down with the waves.

There would be no gators as were in the fresh water but those critters that lived entirely under water, except for the large dorsal fin they seemed to enjoy displaying while following along a few feet from a boat, looked every bit as dangerous as large gator tails. But these were only playful porpoises that would protect a sailor, if overboard, from the long sharks that displayed a much larger fin, but stayed away from the boat because of the porpoises.

About mid-afternoon they located the prong that would lead to the creek and Bruce turned the boat into it, expecting to make camp for the night at the creek's head before starting the search for the poachers.

As he reached the upper end of the creek he could see another boat was tied up at what appeared to be a natural boat landing. The boat was an almost duplicate of their boat and they recognized it. It belonged to a fisherman who lived on the ridge between the Kissimmee River and Tantie, who fished a trotline from this boat near Bruce's fishing water off Buckhead Ridge.

With there being no way to know when the owner would return for the boat, Bruce could not leave their boat there, but would have to find a place to hide it lest it may leave too, when the other boat did.

Not far away they discovered a short, narrow branch off this same creek and by pushing aside overhanging limbs that were hiding its entrance, the boat could squeeze through and was navigated a considerable distance from the main creek by standing and pulling on other limbs. This is not what they had in mind as a camp site, but it had total privacy and their boat was completely hidden from everything but marine life.

Spending the night at the head of the small branch with their boat swallowed up in the mangrove limbs that hung down to the water seemed a serene setting to begin with, but they soon found it everything but private. As the sun settled to the west, relieving the jungle from part of the heat, guests began calling and before night they had to break out the mosquito netting and spread it over the back part of the boat and over the ridge pole as they did with the tarpaulin. Had there been rain during the night, forcing them to use the waterproof cover, they would have been miserable in the close and stuffy jungle.

Sometime before morning they could feel that the boat had listed to a noticeable angle which caused worry until daylight when they could see the cause. The tide had gone out, leaving the boat sitting in the jungle on a black mud flat.

With the water gone from under the boat, reaching land to start their hike was not the problem they first anticipated, and it was not long until they were on their way, trying to find sign leading from the other boat into the jungle toward where Bruce was told he would find the tree snail area. Bruce was carrying the backpack of pup tent, mosquito netting and a food supply that would last for three days, while Fannie followed with the little rifle and a scout ax, with Tag and Varmint at her heels.

The distance between where the boat was left and where the shell poachers were operating was not known, but the sign they had left was bold and seemed to be leading in one straight direction, making following it easy and fast.

Caution was the byword now, lest they stumble upon the camp unexpectedly and flush their quarry, only to hear them run through the thick undergrowth while escaping, rendering the entire trip a waste of time.

Being able to follow the many signs of wilted leaves clinging to tender growth that was unintentionally broken, rotting tree limbs that lay on the ground to be stepped on and show freshly broken, the never ending blobs of tobacco juice spat upon the broad leaves along the trail, and the density of the undergrowth made progress slow.

Pushing through the thick foliage was tiring and they had lunch early, where they left the trail a considerable distance to avoid anyone who may chance to pass during that period.

After having lunch they came back and picked up the signs again to continue the search with hopes of finding the camp before the end of the day. Their hopes were hardly expressed when a low growl came from Tag, where he was following at Fannie's heels. Bruce stopped immediately to watch Tag's actions and try to determine what was bothering him. He heard the sound continue from Tag as he moved around Fannie to slowly come forward with raised bristle and a determined appearance.

Tag passed Bruce to venture on ahead but Bruce knew this would not do. If it was a fearless mother panther with her young kittens, Tag's hide would not hold water when she finished with him, and if it happened to be a big bull gator traveling overland between bodies of water where gators lived...well, this was something that made Bruce shudder to think of. He grabbed Tag and delivered him to Fannie to hold while he crept slowly forward to investigate, leaving Tag having conniptions as he tried to free himself to follow.

Bruce was on his hands and knees and had gone only a short distance when he heard grunting, snarling and squealing coming from a short distance ahead. This demanded more caution as Bruce crept closer to see a small black bear enjoying berries she was picking from tall bushes while standing on her back feet, with her two cubs playfully wrestling in the dry leaves nearby.

After gleefully watching the natural life activities of the wilds, until they moved on to find other berries, Bruce was ready to move back and join Fannie and Tag, but then he heard other sounds further on. A man yelled and then fouled the air with violent cursing while others could be heard laughing. Bruce could not understand what the men were saying but he knew this was the camp and he thanked the bear cubs for attracting Tag's attention before they walked unannounced, and definitely unintentionally, into enemy headquarters.

Even though the sun was only slightly over the top, they would have to await another day, so now was the time for Bruce to pull back quietly to find a campsite beyond the sounds coming from the poachers' camp.

A suitable sight was found and when camp was set up, with the tent erected and Tag on a leash tethered to a stout tree near the tent, Bruce checked the rifle to make sure Fannie would have protection while he was gone before he left her and Tag to go scout the poacher's camp for information before night. They had left Varmint at the boat because he liked to run wild, but he always appeared again when they were ready to travel.

What made Fannie do it, she did not know. But when Bruce was well on his way she loosed Tag's leash from the tree and tied it around her waist, then set out very slowly as Tag tugged at his end of the leash with his nose to the ground on Bruce's trail.

With the day only half gone there was no need to

hurry and, after hearing voices again, Bruce knew he was close, causing him to slow his pace to that of a tortoise.

Some of the voices Bruce heard sounded familiar but he was not able to place them. Then after moving closer he quickly learned who one of the voices belonged to, by having it startle him from a few feet away when the man yelled to his buddies, "Hey, Luke! Tim! Here is old Bruce Coggins, alias, Burl Collins! I bet he has come to work with us!"

The sincere tone of the man's voice and seeing who it was coming from were confusing to Bruce — a few days ago the man was searching for Bruce to turn him in, with the hundred dollar reward in mind.

The other two men pushed through the thick growth then, but not to see a stranger. They were very well acquainted with Bruce and seemed amused and delighted at his showing up, now at their mercy in this remote jungle.

If their friend thought Bruce came to help them with the shell business, he was the only one who did. Luke, the largest one of the group answered his friend with, "Buck, you know what it is like to be a free man! You served your time, but old Bruce here, he escaped so long ago that he thinks he is free too, and now he has turned against his old buddies. He got the drop on Tim and me in Fort Myers and pinned us down until the law arrived! Bucky Boy, you don't know this skunk like we do! He ain't here to help! He's planning to take us in!...if he can!"

As Luke talked, his growing anger was obvious, making his voice practically a scream before he finished the last statement. But his enjoyment of having Bruce here made him go further to torture Bruce more, then he turned and beckoned Bruce to follow.

Luke waded back through the thick foliage with Tim at his heels and Buck following Bruce, until they reached a small area clear of undergrowth that was completely shaded with large banyan trees, making a cool, cozy campsite. Evidently, this was their permanent headquarters, with a newly-constructed thatch hut that would shed at least part of the rain as well as the embers of many campfires outside. To one side sat several pails covered with canvas.

It was the pails that Luke was wanting to show Bruce. He pulled the cover off the pails and invited his prisoner to "Cast your double-crossing eyes on these jewels, you skunk!"

The pails contained small multi-colored shells of the tree snail, and nearby more of the shells lay spread out on the ground where the mollusk had been punctured to kill it and placed there for the large wood ants to clean the shell out.

With anger building up in Luke's every word, Bruce knew the showdown was near and who he would have to be most careful of. Bruce was not ready. He hoped for this to come early tomorrow morning, but sometimes things don't work as planned and he would have to play it by ear now.

No sounds but those coming from the jungle could be heard. There was a stillness that seemed strange, while tension could be felt in the air. The other two men were quietly milling about, seeking a position for action, or to be out of it, maybe.

Luke and Bruce stood immobile with their eyes fixed on each other for a long time, with each trying to anticipate the other's move and thoughts. Bruce could see hate and determination slowly building up in Luke's eyes and knew the time was short. He waited until the breaking point was only a split second away, then he fell and rolled at the same time, and somehow during this movement the little Owls Head revolver appeared in his left hand. Luke had started to draw too and would have been ahead of Bruce but Bruce's unusual actions confused and slowed him, making that his mistake. The report of the two guns sounded as one, and what was impossible to happen, did happen — two hunks of lead met head on in mid air, shattering each other, with the fragments falling to the ground.

Frustration was tremendous as Luke wondered why he did not hit Bruce, with Bruce not able to understand how he missed such a large target as the pistol in Luke's hand. But the time they spent in amazement was not all that long because, from a few feet in the thick growth at Luke's side, the little rifle cracked and Tag was lunging forward even before Luke's gun reached the ground at his feet. Tag continued his work by running on through to grab the gun and come to stand beside Bruce.

Through the last breathtaking seconds the other men made no effort to draw and Bruce was not sure they were armed, but when Fannie came to stand beside him with her rifle trained on Luke, Bruce swung his revolver towards the other two men and ordered them to drop their guns. To Bruce's surprise they both pulled hand guns from their pockets and dropped them on the ground. Tag thought this was a "fetch" game. He ran to each man and brought the guns to Bruce's feet.

Bruce's teaching Fannie how to use the rifle had surely paid off, but Luke did not know this was a single shot rifle and would be about as effective as a stick if he decided to duck through the bushes and escape, because Fannie had forgotten to reload the rifle.

The large trees were hiding the sun but Bruce knew

it was just over the top on the afternoon side and it would be too long a time to hold these men here until tomorrow. He announced to all concerned that a midnight party was in the offing. They were all headed for Fort Myers immediately.

Bruce rapidly snapped orders as he rushed about where he handcuffed the men together and gave each one a pail of the snail shells. Then, with two pails left, he and Fannie picked them up and the party set out briskly back toward the boats.

When they reached the tent, which they did not use, they saw Varmint for the first time since the shooting began. He emerged slowly from the tent where he had been hiding. Bruce repacked the tent and swung it across his back, picked up a pail of shells again and they were off with only a couple minutes delay. With Tag's sensitive nose keeping them on course, they were able to travel faster than when coming in, and were at the boats in short order.

During the hike back to the boats Bruce was in a quandary about the boats being separated and if the tide was too low to get his boat out of the shallow branch. But upon reaching the creek and finding the tide about the way it was when they came in, Bruce ordered everyone into the poacher's boat, and by everyone pulling on low hanging mangrove limbs it was drawn up the branch to Bruce's boat, where a line was fastened and both boats brought out together. Everyone changed boats then and the poacher's boat was placed in tow behind Bruce's boat.

With the three prisoners ahead of the engine box and Fannie, Varmint, Tag and Bruce at the stern, the faithful little engine began biting water with its oversize propeller.

146

Bruce knew the route out to the main channel and they were in it headed for Fort Myers when darkness began having its way. Although the engine was beating steady and shaking the boat, the best it could with every stroke, they were not traveling as fast now with the boat in tow.

There was concern about the men easing themselves over the side, one at the time, after darkness set in, and swimming away. But now, if leaving the handcuffs on them did not dampen that possibility, the several large shark fins that were seen near the boat before dark certainly would have some effect.

Other than the prisoners trying to scare Bruce into releasing them with the threat of exposing him as an escapee himself, where he too would be sent back to Raiford, Bruce had no trouble with them.

The prisoners argued among themselves the entire way but what they were arguing about was not known. With the popping noise of the steady engine exhaust, their words were not understood. It was thought the men were hatching some kind of an escape attempt and the only thing keeping them from trying it was the fear of the rifle in Fannie's hands and the smooth little revolver that seemed to appear in Bruce's left hand by magic. To Bruce's surprise there was no attempted escape while in the boat and they reached Fort Myers before midnight.

The Sheriff had just arrived back from a night call and was in the jailer's office when the three prisoners followed by their captors entered the office. The Sheriff expressed surprise at the job being done so quickly. Bruce's party had been gone from town less than forty-eight hours.

But there was not much time for the Sheriff to talk about his surprise before Bucky Boy attempted to put in his two cents worth and justify his being with the shell poachers with, "Here is your man, Sheriff! Bruce Coggins! The man who escaped Raiford, and now is using the name of Burl Collins! I told you I would find him and use some kind of ruse to bring him in! I did too! I made him think I was working with these two other ex-cons! A pretty good trick, eh, Sheriff?"

"A pretty good trick is right, Buck! But not quite good enough! Why were you traveling in a stolen boat when you came through here with that cock-and-bull story about you knowing where these two escapees were holing up, and you were going to work a gimmick to get them captured? And that you would split the reward with me if I advanced you half then!"

Buck was wishing now that he had remained quiet, and attempting to clear himself with his buddies, he sputtered, "But Sheriff, I'm a free man! I served all my time and was released! And my two good buddies here know I was one of them and would not let them down!"

"Buck, you are using the wrong word! You 'was' free but not since the fisherman from the upper end of the lake was in here after you left to report his boat stolen, and too, since Burl found you living in the shell poacher's camp!"

It seemed the more Buck tried to explain, the less trusting he found his buddies, not to mention the brand the Sheriff was applying to his hide.

Through all this big Luke was silent but not blank. His cunning brain was working double time. He was the only one who saw the revolver under some papers in a tray on the jailer's desk which the Sheriff was sitting behind. And now with all the talk between Buck and the Sheriff going on, Luke was not noticed as he kept inching his way towards that corner of the desk.

148

Luke was hitched to Buck with handcuffs on the side next to the gun and when he thought he was close enough to reach it without having to drag Buck as an anchor, he made a quick grab, and lightening fast the gun was leveled at the Sheriff. With Luke directly between Bruce and the Sheriff, it was not possible for Bruce to do any firing. Bruce noticed that the Sheriff was just sitting there in a frozen-like manner. Then a slow smile began developing on the Sheriff's face, but he still did not move. Luke saw this and knew, somehow, he had failed, before the Sheriff calmly stated, "Luke, I hope you don't think the jailer would be careless enough to leave a loaded gun lying around for the taking!"

Knowing now the reason for the Sheriff's smile, Luke placed the gun gently on the desk top and was backing away as the Sheriff finished the statement. Then the Sheriff picked up the revolver and turned out the cylinder to have six live loads drop out and onto the desk top.

Then with no further ado, the Sheriff took the jail keys from the desk drawer, arose and pointed to the cell block where the handcuffs were removed and the men pushed into a cell — not before a complete search was made, including their shoes for saw blades or weapons. After a moment's thought, the Sheriff opened the cell again and called Buck, placing him in another cell.

After a short visit with the Sheriff, being congratulated as "Burl" and "Frances" for a job well done, while petting Tag for his part, the Sheriff heard Bruce beg for no more assignments for awhile and express his desires to be on his way home. The Sheriff then went into his own office and made "Burl" and "Frances" a check in payment for this job, while trying to get a promise from Bruce for more jobs later.

Now, with his hand extended for the parting, the Sheriff stated, "Frances! Burl! It is people like you who give law officers a new lease on life...a further confidence in their fellow man!" The Sheriff knew there would be no reply and he turned abruptly to go back into the jailer's office as Bruce and Fannie waved while going out the door.

They slept in the boat tied up at the town dock for a few hours, then headed up the river with the stolen boat in tow at daybreak.

When passing the net racks, Bruce stood with the tiller stick between his knees, hoping in this position he would be able to see his friends. But no one was at the net racks. There still was no market for their fish.

With the sun climbing through the tree tops in the east burning out the fog that had settled on the water during the night, the business of navigating the swift river with another boat in tow, while trying to avoid colliding with other craft coming down which might be out of control due to the current, was utmost in Bruce's thoughts.

Not being able to see his friends when passing the net racks was disappointing to Bruce, but he dismissed that and settled down for the job ahead and the long journey back to Buckhead Ridge.

They were in the narrow and swift river now, with the old heavy slugging boat engine pounding steadily, with the foliage along the river's banks slowly passing, then disappearing behind.

With he and Fannie sitting quietly in deep thought, watching Tag and Varmint frolic on the floor of the boat, and seemingly with nothing better to do, Bruce drew the folded check from his pocket to learn how much the Sheriff had paid them for their work. The check was made payable to Bruce and Fannie Coggins.